BLESS ME FATHER

LOU SAULINO

Lou Creative

imagination not imitation

Published in the United States of America
ISBN: 978-1-953904-86-7 (SC)
ISBN: 978-1-955243-10-0 (Ebook)

Lou Saulino Publishing
222 West 6th Street
Suite 400, San Pedro, CA, 90731
www.loucreativeinc.com
Order Information and Rights Permission:

Quantity sales. Special discounts might be available on quantity purchases by corporations, associations, and others. For details, contact the publisher at the address above.
For Book Rights Adaptation and other Rights Permission. Call us at toll-free 1-888-945-8513 or send us an email at admin@stellarliterary.com.

For Emily Grace,
and in loving memory of Maryann,
who is watching over her.

CONTENTS

Introduction

Sports historical fiction is a unique Brand. The integration of family, friendship, and my life experiences was envisioned as a style which would identify me as a writer. Three of four Published works, a trilogy of the continuing saga of three best friends since childhood, with settings commencing in the late nineteen fifties and progressing into the ninth decade of the twentieth century, followed this technique.

"8" Centerfield in New York, 1951-1957 was the inauguration of the concept, the account of the baseball exploits of Willie Mays, Mickey Mantle and Duke Snider told through the eyes of three thirteen year old best friends in 1957. ***Dopey Bastid*** followed and depicted the progression of the three comrades into adulthood, and coupled the review of dumb decisions in the sports world through the accounts of one of the three friends, now a sportswriter for the New York Daily News. The chronicle of sports and friendship concluded with ***FRAMILY (friends considered family)***, as the three good buddies have now all reconnected with their childhood mates and started families.

Kirkus Reviews has been impressed.

- "Saulino is a talented story teller. And the way he mixes nostalgic sports stories with those of the group of friends is smart and inventive ***(Dopey Bastid).***"
- "Readers needn't be sports fans to enjoy the work ***(FRAMILY)***; even those who are athletically challenged will be gripped by what is, at its heart, a tale of love."
- "the book ***(FRAMILY)*** is also immaculately researched , vividly recalling each play of each game like a great sports announcer."

A fourth book, **Athlete For Hire,** explored the fictional travails of a creative sports team owner to sign a college phenom, proficient in baseball, football and basketball, to play for all three of his professional sports franchises. This novel was originally written as a TV Pilot and is also being promoted for the big screen.

So now we come to **Bless Me Father**. Why the Brand modification? Hey, what the hell do I know? My professional background is civil engineering and I continue to practice on an executive level. A mystery, with just a minor backdrop into sports, just seemed the way to expand my reading audience.

I realized that it would be helpful to seek advice and a review by those outside of my inner circle of family and friends; and was quite fortunate to have intuitive input from a former Roman Catholic priest and two law enforcement professionals. A special thank you to Peter Olsinski , John Sullivan, an old friend and retired New York City Police Department Detective, and Cecile Woodward, the former Assistant Police Chief of the Phoenix Police Department. Thank you guys for the astute comments and suggestions from your personal life experiences.

The highly positive appraisal by KIRKUS REVIEW emboldened me, as did comments from a friend and working associate, Julia Schneider. "I devoured the book and it was delicious. The author has a real talent for character development. Just a few chapters in and I was emotionally invested in the cast."

Chapter I

Angela Bella

1

St. Patrick's Day 1987

Anthony "Tony" Calabrese and his soon-to-be fiancée, Angela Santino, approached Bay Ridge Liquors in Tony's 1984 Chevy Camaro. The Brooklyn, New York, establishment was midblock among an eclectic array of stores in the west end of Bay Ridge, a mere half a mile from the Verrazano Bridge.

"You are not being truthful with me, Tony. You love this freakin' car more than me."

Angela was not serious but loved to get under Tony's skin regarding his affection for the Z28, which *Car and Driver* had picked as the best handling car built in the United States.

"C'mon, Angela, enough with the jealousy toward my four-wheeled girlfriend. We have a different kind of relationship."

"Yeah, sure, Italian Stallion. The car will probably get a ring from you before I will. You got your wish with the Giants winning the Super Bowl, and yet Valentine's Day has come and gone. What are you waiting for now, the Rangers to win the Stanley Cup?"

"Shit, there is no parking here. Take my credit card and go in and get a few bottles for my brother-in-law and sister. Get a bottle of Jameson's. Sully makes a great Irish coffee with it. Maria also said to bring a bottle of wine."

"What kind of wine?"

"Valpolicella. It goes perfect with corned beef," added Tony, grinning. "I'm going to drive around a bit. The cops around here are not appreciative of double-parking. I'll meet you in front in about ten minutes."

"OK, my love. Think about the ring, though, at least one carat and either a pear shaped or round stone, size 7. And remember, you have to get down on your knees to propose, and it better be romantic."

"You haven't gotten down on your knees yet."

Angela understood the sexual connotation of her smirking boyfriend.

"Maybe for your birthday, but you will need a note from your mother confirming her permission."

"Yeah right!"

Upon exiting the car, Angela noticed a red Mustang with an It's Miller Time bumper sticker and Miller Time coasters along the rear dashboard.

"I like this car, Tony, check it out. Do you want me to pick up beer too?"

"No, Hoops, my sister said they had plenty."

Angela blew Tony a kiss and entered the store, just as an older gentleman was leaving and held the door open for her.

Tony perused the red Mustang but felt that it fell short of his metallic-black Chevy Camaro. A honking horn precipitated his shifting from Park to Drive, and he passed a jewelry store before stopping at a traffic light on the corner. After making a right turn, he pulled over by a fire hydrant and took out the small notepad and pen from the glove compartment. The viewing of Patricia's Jewelry Shop had refocused his attention. The time for dragging his feet on placing an engagement ring on the finger of Angela Santino had run out. The reminder to himself simply read, "Pear shaped or round, size 7."

Less than fifteen minutes later, amid the sound of police sirens, the Camaro approached the liquor store. Two police cars were now double-parked in front with lights flashing. Tony drove past the second of the two NYPD vehicles, shut off the engine, and hurriedly exited, proceeding toward the front entrance of Bay Ridge Liquors. He was detained by one of several police officers at the scene.

"What's going on? You have to let me through, Officer, my girlfriend is in there."

2

Virtually four hundred family and friends were in attendance to say good-bye to the fiancée-to-be of Anthony Calabrese, the loving daughter of Mary and Sal Santino.

The three days prior to the funeral Mass, one awaiting the release of Angela's body from the medical examiner and two at the funeral parlor, had gone by abruptly. Memories of the tall, athletic, vivacious, and alluring college senior were emotional. Angela's tragic murder, a month and a half shy of her twenty-second birthday, was unresolved. The police had no eyewitnesses. Discussion with Tony yielded little in the way of a lead.

The *New York Daily News*, *New York Times*, and *New York Post* all carried stories about the tragedy; the *Daily News* added an acknowledgement in the sports section.

> March 19, 1987
> College Sports
>
> Angela Santino, star guard on the Manhattan College Lady Jaspers basketball team, was tragically killed during a liquor store robbery in Bay Ridge, Brooklyn, on St. Patrick's Day. The MAAC Conference first team All-Star led her team in points per game and assists. Angela was considered a strong candidate to compete for a spot on the 1988 USA Olympic women's basketball team.

Angela had a copious and close-knit family. It was a painful experience, particularly for her mother and father; she was their only child. The mourners included old friends from the Bronx, where she grew up; her admirers from Christ the King High School in Middle Village, Queens; and the college contingent of those individuals construed to be much more than mere acquaintances. Her acclaim as an all-city basketball player in high school and all-conference status in the Metro Atlantic Athletic Conference as a stellar guard for Manhattan College filled the pews with an anguished populace. Faculty from both high school and college, and even Sisters Elizabeth Marie and Josephine from her seventh and eighth grade Catholic grammar school, attended the funeral service.

Tony's family, universally fond of Angela, were tearful in the loss of the girl who they knew would soon become a Calabrese. Tony's friends from the neighborhood, his Manhattan College baseball teammates, and many mutual admirers of Angela and Tony were there to support the departed black-haired beauty and the sentimental Italian.

Father Carlos was remorseful yet ebullient in his homily. He had met Angela through Tony some three years prior. Angela and Tony had always identified their preference for him to perform their inevitable wedding ceremony. He never thought his presence would be required to welcome Angela into God's hands. He stressed her family values, love of life, and what he saw as a relationship with Tony that was based on mutual respect and sincerity.

After a heartfelt ten minutes, Father Carlos concluded his thoughts. "I first met Angela through Tony several years ago, but it seems like I have known her forever. Tony confided in me often about his love for her. 'She is the one, Father.'"

The priest paused momentarily. "Tony has asked if he could say a few words about Angela. C'mon up, Anthony."

Tony had been cognizant that his time to speak was imminent. Moments before Father Carlos requested his presence at the pulpit, he swallowed the contents of the small flask he had brought with him. The Johnnie Walker Black Label from his dad's stock was the elixir he hoped would quell his anguish and afford him with the opportunity to pay tribute to Angela without breaking down. The sincerity in his voice was palpable. "Angela was a special person, but you guys already knew that. I wanted to share a few stories with you, though, and then read the poem I have written for her.

"So how did the two of us meet? Well, in my freshman year at Manhattan College, I was screwing around on the basketball court at Van Cortlandt Park. I was practicing free throws in preparation of an intramural game. I was a pretty good shooter, at least I thought so. Angela walked by with one of her girlfriends."

He looked into the throng of her admirers and pointed toward an attractive blond-haired female.

"Do you remember, Michelle?"

After acknowledging Angela's basketball teammate, Tony continued.

"Well, anyway, she comes over to me as I am shooting and questions my form.

"'That's no way to shoot a foul shot. I've seen you pitch, and baseball is obviously your sport. Leave the basketball playing to my friend Michelle over there and me.'

"I could not help but smile and was obviously intrigued. She was beautiful, tall, and sassy.

"I rebutted her comment. 'Is that right?' I said. 'Would you care to bet that if we both attempt ten shots that you will be sobbing like a little girl who just dropped her ice cream cone on the ground after I beat your butt? How about loser buys dinner, whatever your name is?'

"I remember her smile and the gleam in her brown eyes as she answered me. 'It's Angela. I already know who you are, the guy who hopes to someday pitch like Tom Seaver. It's Tony, right?'

"Then she laughed and accepted the wager. My competitive spirit was brewing. I couldn't wait to wipe that smirk off her face.

"After making eight of ten shots, I was pretty confident that I had at least earned a tie with the confident lass. Without a word, I just grinned and handed her the basketball. I said something like, 'OK, Magic, you're up.'

"Angela changed her expression. It was almost as if she was putting her game face on. 'Just give me the ball, good-lookin'. By the way, my favorite place for dinner is Luigi's in Jackson Heights. My dad is good friends with the owner.'

"She then proceeded to make nine free throws in a row.

What a crock. She didn't even need her last shot. After passing me the ball back, she corrected my use of the name Magic for her. 'My free throw percentage is better than Magic Johnson's, closer to Larry Bird's,' she said."

Tony was now smiling broadly as he continued his discourse. The memory of his first meeting with Angela had put him at ease. Almost all in the congregation were chuckling.

"I should add that we had a great time at Luigi's restaurant. Appetizers with a cocktail, main course with a bottle of wine, dessert with espresso, and then an after-dinner drink. It wasn't cheap. She offered to leave the tip. 'No way, Hoops,' I said. That was the first nickname I had for her."

Tony continued with a second story about a poem he was studying in a sophomore English literature class. Lord Byron's "She Walks in Beauty." Angela had mistakenly thought that the poem was written by John Keats.

"I corrected her. 'You just stick with basketball, Hoops, that's what you do best.'"

The joviality ceased as Anthony Calabrese began one final recollection; his demeanor was a paradigm of authenticity. "My grandmother Rosa is no longer with us. May she rest in peace. I bring her up to identify how intuitive she was regarding the quality of a person. She had a sixth sense and was rarely, if ever, wrong. The first time I introduced Angela to her, it didn't take her long to pull me aside. 'I lika her, Anthony, maka sure you be nice.' Well, soon thereafter, whenever she referred to Angela, it was never just Angela, it was Angela Bella.

"I have written a poem for Angela and would like to share it with you. It is entitled 'Angela Bella.'"

A deep breath and a quick wipe of a cascading tear preceded Tony's rhyming verse. It was intended to be tender with a touch of humor. He prayed that Mr. and Mrs. Santino would find his words satisfactory. He looked briefly at his mother before commencing and was comforted by the warmth of her smile.

> *She walks in beauty like the night,*
> *Byron's words fit her well; Angela was truly a*
>   *beautiful sight.*
> *She was caring, intelligent, athletic and funny,*
> *Always there for others, and with a disposition*
>   *sunny.*
> *My soul mate, the love of my life, a best friend*
>   *for sure,*
> *When I was down, her glowing smile was the*
>   *cure.*
> *Angela only had two faults, rooting for the*
>   *Islanders and Mets,*
> *Thank God her football interests were with the*
>   *Giants, not Jets.*
> *So as I stand before you guys, her family and*
>   *friends,*
> *I ask for forgiveness and hope to somehow*
>   *make amends.*
> *I wish I was the one who had entered the liquor*
>   *store,*
> *She should be here with you today and many*
>   *years more.*
> *Good bye my love, I will forever be your fella,*
> *Rest in peace my sweet, my 'Angela Bella'.*

Tony immediately broke down after his tribute to the girl he expected to spend the rest of his life with. Thoughts of letting her enter the liquor store without him and having procrastinated regarding giving her an engagement ring haunted the popular and sincere speaker.

Father Carlos went over to him and kissed him on the forehead. As Tony walked from the pulpit back to his seat, he was intercepted by Angela's parents. The heartfelt hugs from her mom and dad provided him solace.

Chapter II

Subway Series

1

October 18, 2000

Father Anthony Calabrese, Father Tony to his parishioners at St. John the Baptist Church, placed flowers on the grave of Angela Santino. His visits to the cemetery were frequent, even now, well over a decade after her tragic demise.

Two additional life-altering events fostered his eventual ordination as a Catholic priest in 1993. His dad, Nicholas, a mere three weeks after Angela was murdered, was diagnosed with pancreatic cancer. Two months later, Tony tearfully spoke at his funeral Mass. He was never able to grieve as openly as he was wont to do. The need to be a comforting son to Teresa Calabrese and his sister, Maria, was his primary obligation.

Tony Calabrese idolized his father, who was seemingly always there for him. He was thankful of the countless times he had played catch with his dad in the driveway of their Queens home, attended ball games at Yankee Stadium, and marveled at how his father could always solve any math problem he had in grammar school and high school. He was astounded by the unselfishness of Nicholas Calabrese. Just prior to his death, his principal concern remained to be his wife, daughter, and son. The day before he closed his eyes for the final time, he reminded Tony of the tenets of a good life. "Be respectful of your elders, make the best use of your God-given talent, and most importantly, always be there for your family."

Several weeks before the loss of the man he so admired, Anthony Calabrese learned that a rotator cuff injury would shut him down just a week before he was to pitch for Manhattan College in their first game of the 1987 College World Series. The prognosis was that in all likelihood, he would never regain the stellar pitching form that had him projected to be selected within the top twenty-five picks of the 1987 baseball draft. His surgery was postponed until after his father was gone, and the diagnosis proved to be prescient.

The six-foot-two-inch, 195-pound heart throb, at least so dubbed by Angela's girlfriends, was emotionally drained and sought avenues that he had never previously traversed. Several months of aimless carousing and drinking ensued. One-night stands became commonplace for the dark-brown-haired womanizer. His friends were concerned; he was not the guy they had all come to know and respect. One bartender at an establishment he frequented commented, "Tony is getting more ass than a toilet seat."

One evening, unbeknownst to Tony, his mom invited Father Carlos for dinner. The dialogue with the priest he had befriended many years before stimulated an epiphany. One week later, after careful reflection, and to the surprise of family and friends, Tony decided to enroll at Catholic University in Washington, DC, to consider the priesthood. He struggled with his fidelity to the Catholic faith, but he ultimately completed his vocation and received his masters of divinity (MDiv) at the Duke Divinity School.

Tony became a very popular ambassador of the Catholic faith. He garnered a reputation of being involved, particularly with youth sports activities, administering to the sick and elderly, and was the go-to priest for hearing confession. Additionally, with the permission of the parish pastor, Father Tony held periodic bereavement meetings in the church auditorium for individuals grieving the loss of a loved one.

Father Tony remained true to his vows, although adhering to his promise of celibacy was a concern. The temptation to resist several of the attractive single women in the parish who ogled him was constant.

Tony cleared the grave site area and placed a fresh bouquet of flowers. He envisioned the radiant smile of the girl he intended to become his wife. His thoughts were momentarily interrupted by the sound of a police car siren; it brought back memories he didn't care to think about. Then, as was his custom, Tony perused the inscription on the tombstone.

Angela Teresa Santino
May 4, 1965–March 17, 1987
Loving Daughter of Mary and Sal
Forever in Our Hearts
"Angela Bella"

The fact that Angela's parents had used the name that Tony's grandmother had coined and that he chose as the title of his funeral eulogy poem never ceased to produce tears to his brown eyes.

"Hey there, Hoops. Can you imagine how we would be fighting if you were down here with me? It will be your Mets against my Yankees starting on Saturday. I'll bet you my boys bring home the bacon for the third year in a row. I'm praying that it won't be like our first bet when you had my number on the basketball court."

He refrained from crying as he continued speaking with his departed soul mate as if she were there with him.

"I still can't believe that you are not here with me. It's been over thirteen years, and I still think about you every day."

Tony paused and then put his hand on the gravestone. "OK, Hoops, so I guess you know why I need your prayers now more than ever. This vow of chastity is getting tougher and tougher. The temptation dealing with flirtatious women is unceasing. The memories of having your legs wrapped around me comforts me. What can I say, being celibate was never in my plans."

Father Anthony Calabrese looked skyward and made one last request before departing.

"Lord, give me the strength to fulfill my vows."

2

That Saturday, as the one remaining penitent began with the customary "Bless me, Father, for I have sinned," an enthralling aroma, reminiscent to him of Angela, pervaded the confessional. The perfume of Mrs. Beverly Thomas, the mother of one of the young boys he coached in the twelve- to fourteen-year-old baseball travel league, was a scent he recognized. She was a frequent attendee at the games and was often accompanied by a buxom, enticing blond friend.

What he was about to hear, however, was unexpected. The identification of many of the typical transgressions of Catholics was followed by a sobbing account of despair. After listening to the wife-beating scenario she was routinely faced with, Tony was momentarily at a loss for an appropriate response. This became even more of an issue after the acknowledgement, "He even hit my son last night when he came to my defense. I wanted to kill him, Father."

Tony was able to console and comfort her but realized this was a situation that required further intervention. He encouraged her to call the rectory and make an appointment to see him that Monday. Beverly (he preferred to think of her by her first name) indicated she would think about it.

Five minutes later, his priestly duties fulfilled for the day, Tony sat in the last pew of the church with his good friend George. He gladly accepted the $550 in winnings from the prior week's football and baseball wagers. The Giants covering the spread against the Cowboys with a fourth quarter touchdown and the Yankees American League Championship Series triumph over the Seattle Mariners were the keys to increasing his profits for the season.

Tony never thought of gambling as a vice; for him, it was just a form of entertainment, similar to how he thought of his drinking. He was a "social" drinker.

George, his Jewish friend since childhood, was the Father Tony intermediary with the bookie who took his wagers.

"So who do you like this week, Tony?"

"It's Yankees time, George, no football bets. Just give me the Yanks. You said I could get even money if I took my boys to win in six games or less, right?"

"That's correct, Father. Damn, I love to call you father. Maybe I should convert."

"No way, my good friend. Your mom, dad, and rabbi would all have heart attacks."

"Yeah, you have a point. So how much are you wagering that the Yankees will, as Pat Riley coined, threepeat?"

"Give me the Bronx Bombers for a grand and I'll take Andy Pettitte to start us off tonight for $300. What will that return, about $200?"

"You'll win $180 on a $300 bet, Tony. By the way, Leiter could give your boys trouble in game 1. He knows how to pitch, and rarely do you see him giving in to the hitter, but good luck. I really have no rooting interest. I'll just continue to root for the Giants. I had them against the Cowboys last week also."

"First of all, the Yankees batters are very patient. They'll take a walk if Leiter doesn't want to come over the plate. Secondly, the Giants have a bye tomorrow, so you can root for the Yanks with me."

"When it comes to sports, you never miss a beat. Do you ever think about what the future would have brought if you didn't have that injury to your pitching arm? Damn, you were a marvel on the mound."

"Many times. But I've been blessed in other ways and have learned to focus on the positives in my life. Listen, buddy, say hello to your parents for me."

3

Father Tony watched game 1 of the World Series in his room at the rectory. He was scheduled to serve at the eight o'clock Mass the following morning and felt it would be more appropriate to stay put. He was satisfied with the fact that he would be able to watch game 2 with his family on Sunday.

The sports enthusiast and avid Yankees fan observed the announcement of the starting lineups for the opening game of the Subway Series.

Tony was quite familiar with the Yankees starting lineup and concentrated on a review of the rival team from his hometown borough of Queens. He felt strongly that Mike Piazza would cause the foremost anxiety for Andy Pettitte and the entire Yankees pitching staff and that controlling the right-handed power hitter would be a key to the Yankees winning their twenty-sixth World Series.

He thought about how he would have tried to contain the Mets All-Star had his pitching career not come to an abrupt end. "Fastballs in, sliders down and away, and keep the change up below the knees. Mix in an occasional slow curve to keep him off balance."

Angela had been an ardent Mets fan. Father Tony recollected her excitement when the Mets became World Series Champions during the fall prior to her premature passing. She was very clear with her boyfriend before the commencement of the '86 Series. "You had better root for my team, Tony, or you'll be logging a lot more innings with that right hand of yours."

The aftermath of the Mets sixth game miraculous come-from-behind victory against the Red Sox came to mind. The scampering of Ray Knight across home plate as the Mookie Wilson ground ball squeezed through the legs of Bill Buckner had Angela in a frenzy; she was a very, very happy lady and showed it in the bedroom that evening. Many of the sexual fantasies of the Italian Stallion were fulfilled before sunset. The priest looked at the picture on his wall. It was a present from Angela and depicted the New York Mets ballplayer she once had dinner with before meeting Tony, Keith Hernandez. The All- Star Mets first baseman was seen prior to the instigation of the '86 World Series shaking hands with the All-Star third baseman of the Boston Red Sox, Wade Boggs.

Father Tony had retained a copy of the handwritten note from Angela, which he had carefully placed on the wall next to the Hernandez picture. Angela found it humorous; Tony's amusement was initially void, but he soon recanted with the realization that Angela was just trying to playfully get under his skin. "Remember, Tony, you better be prepared to commit to our relationship, or I'll have to call Keith and have him take your place."

Tony was in ecstasy after the repeat performance of Hoops in her apartment two days later, the evening of the culmination of the Mets 1986 World Series quest. He recalled using a line that he had never uttered before or ever again, "Let's go, Mets." Father Anthony Calabrese had the confession of Beverly Thomas on his mind as the first pitch of the New York City Subway Series was thrown at 8:13 p.m.

Father Tony began thinking about his wager on the Series and his individual bet on the first game. He stood to lose $300 on the first-game wager, and the $1,000 bet that the Yankees would win the Series in six games or less would obviously be in serious jeopardy if the opening game outcome was favorable to the National League team, who were viewed as the replacement for the two stalwart franchises that had absconded to the West Coast in 1957, the Giants and Dodgers.

The five hundred shares of Exxon Mobil stock he had inherited from his dad was reinvested wisely, and the priest had a bank account that afforded him with the wherewithal to place wagers despite the minimal salary he received as a parish priest. He was also an astute bettor, with a knowledge of sports far surpassing the majority of the so-called experts.

The Yankees trailed the Mets 3–2 entering the bottom of the ninth inning at the House That Ruth Built. The team, often described by Tony as the pinstripe machine, tied the encounter in that inning and then pushed across a run in the twelfth for a 4–3 victory.

As he lay in bed, prior to focusing on his morning homily, the elation of the Yankees' victory was suppressed by thoughts of the confession of Beverly Thomas. It was comforting to him as a priest, and more imperatively as a person, that his intercession regarding the problem of one of his parishioners was just as important to him as the fate of the Yankees.

4

"Well, it's obvious the Lord is a Yankees fan."

The opening remarks of the priest's sermon had the majority of the eight o'clock Mass parishioners displaying broad smiles. Of course, that was except for the Mets fans.

Later that day, Tony arrived at the two-story home where he grew up in the borough of Queens. He still had a bedroom in the first-floor abode occupied by his mom. The second floor of the brick-faced edifice was the living quarters for his sister, Maria, her husband, Johnny, and the twins, Tammy and Tommy. Tony was truly grateful for his family. He knew that it if not for his mom, dad, and sister, he would never have recovered from the loss of Angela. Soon thereafter, the closeness between his mom, his sister, and himself was the antidote to suppress the sorrow of his father succumbing to pancreatic cancer.

With the Giants on a bye week and the Yankees-Mets World Series his primary concern, Tony had abstained from his customary Sunday pro football wagering. Football, however, was discussed at the dining room table, Tony emphatic about telling his Jets fan brother-in-law that the verdant and white was still the second-best team in New York to Big Blue. It was not easy to prove, however. The Jets, who already had their bye week, stood at 5–1 and were scheduled to face the Dolphins on *Monday Night Football*; the Giants were 5–2.

Teresa Calabrese, Tony's mom, now a widow for over thirteen years, was sixty-one years of age. She remained a vibrant and beautiful woman. Mrs. Calabrese treated her Anthony like royalty, particularly enthralled with every opportunity to cook for him. That Sunday, her menu called for manicotti, with meatballs and sausage, followed by a beef roast with potatoes and escarole. Of course, this was to be preceded by a cold antipasto platter of salami, prosciutto, provolone cheese, assorted Italian olives, and Italian bread. Dessert would feature her homemade Italian cheesecake and espresso.

Father Tony brought his customary bottle of Valpolicella, a red wine favorite dating back to his time with Angela.

The dinner table was lively with Yankees-Mets talk. It was very one-sided. The Calabrese family was entrenched in a tradition of Yankees baseball. Tony's paternal grandfather was an avid follower of the Italian ballplayers in pinstripes. The exploits of DiMaggio, Rizzuto, and Berra were always of ultimate importance to him, and he passed along the love of the Yankees and these players to his son, Nicholas. In turn, Tony's dad maintained a devotion to the Bronx Bombers and taught Tony all about Yankees history, with a concentration on the Italian player contributions.

Tony and his father often frequented games at Yankee Stadium. His mother and sister would habitually join them.

Father Anthony Calabrese was enamored with the story about his mom, who, after meeting her husband-to-be, Nick, in 1960, created a stir in the family when she began to follow the Yankees. She discussed this at the dinner table.

"It was pretty funny. I thought that I was going to be banned from the Calabrese household. I said that I thought Mickey Mantle must have been as good as or better than Joe DiMaggio. Plus, he was better looking. Mickey was always my favorite."

Maria Sullivan laughed at her mother's identification. "I remember Dad telling me that story. He said the stare you got from his father was more intense than the time he had broken the garage door window playing baseball."

Father Tony was thankful that his mother and sister had stood by him in the aftermath of Angela's death. Each was convinced that she was a perfect complement to Tony. Teresa Calabrese had remarked, "I never thought that there would be a girl good enough for my Anthony, I was wrong."

Maria Sullivan had pronounced to her brother, "You are very lucky to have a woman who is beautiful inside and out. I feel that I will be gaining a sister."

Mother, daughter, and son were a comforting and consoling trio during the cancer treatment and eventual passing of Nick Calabrese.

Johnny Sullivan, whom Maria married in the spring of 1986, was the family baseball outcast. The sole rooter of the team whose stadium was frequented by the sound of Jets departing and arriving from LaGuardia Airport, the Mets, chimed in.

"That reminds me of the movie *A Bronx Tale*. The kid is heaping praise on his idol, Mickey Mantle, and his dad is telling him that DiMaggio was better."

Father Tony thought of Johnny as more than just a brother- in-law. The tall blond-haired Irishman had become his best friend. His admiration for the NYPD Detective was conspicuous. He viewed Johnny as a devoted husband, caring father, and someone he could confide in. The fact that he was a sports enthusiast was an added bonus. When they spoke one-on-one, he often referred to him by the moniker used by his fellow NYPD brethren, Sully.

Before Johnny could add to his movie disclosure, his wife chimed in. "The kid's name was Calogero. I think that was Chazz Palminteri's name in real life."

Then, the family matriarch sought to contribute to the conversation about the movie with Italian heritage recollections from the borough of the Bronx.

"Your father would have loved that movie. Robert De Niro was his favorite actor. The story I heard was that De Niro saw Chazz Palminteri perform *A Bronx Tale* as a one-man show and became interested in working with him to make the movie. Chazz wanted to play the part of the local Mafia boss, Sonny, so De Niro agreed to portray the boy's father. He was also the director of the film."

Tony concluded the discussion about the 1993 movie and then added his thoughts about Mantle.

"You're right, Mom. Dad would have been in his glory watching that story."

Tony was too young to ever see Mantle play. Of course, there was TV footage, and he had read a few books about the Yankees great. He felt inclined to bring up how moved he was reading the tributes to Mickey after he died two months after receiving a liver transplant in 1995.

"It was very obvious that his teammates loved him. That was of ultimate importance to him. The eulogy of Bob Costas was unbelievable. I still have a copy of that."

Tony's childhood idol was Thurman Munson and then as a teenager, as he became an accomplished pitcher and part-time first baseman, Ron Guidry and Don Mattingly.

Maria Sullivan, a year and a half older than her brother, was a Derek Jeter fanatic. Her first Yankees favorite was also a shortstop. As a fifteen-year-old she had a crush on Bucky Dent. The high school English teacher, whom many felt resembled Sophia Loren, remarked about the New York Yankees whom Red Sox fans referred to as Bucky "F———n" Dent.

"He was extremely good-looking. Then, when he hit that home run off Torrez in 1978, he was everybody's hero,"

Maria still retained the framed photo she had received from her dad that Christmas: her Bucky being gleefully greeted by his teammates as he crossed home plate after the historic home run.

Tony added two Yankees history facts.

"You brought up Mike Torrez, which was very ironic. The year before, he was the winning pitcher when the Yankees won their first World Series since 1962. Also, a little bit of trivia: your boy Bucky was the World Series MVP in '78."

Much to the chagrin of Johnny, the rooting interest of his twins were in tune with their grandmother, mother, and uncle Tony. He was not a happy camper with the fact that his daughter and son had each taken on the Yankees banner.

Tammy thought Tino Martinez was "so, so handsome," while Tommy, an outfielder in the youth leagues, favored Bernie Williams and Paul O'Neill.

Johnny Sullivan felt the need to defend his position as the lone dissenter of the team his father had taught him to despise. "Hey, my dad was a Brooklyn Dodger fan and then became a Mets advocate when they arrived in Queens. My blood is blue and orange. Pop taught me about the great Dodger teams with Duke Snider, Roy Campanella, Gil Hodges, Pee Wee Reese, and Jackie Robinson."

"They were very good but only got the upper hand on the Yankees in 1955," added his sports-knowledgeable wife.

"Well, they had some exceptional teams in Brooklyn, and let me add that I think the 1986 Mets team was one of the best teams of all time. Hernandez, Carter, Strawberry, and Gooden, c'mon, you guys, they were great."

As Tony passed the platter of manicotti to Johnny, he postulated about the previous night's Yankees victory. "Posada's double was the key. That moved Tino to third with only one out." "Yeah, but Wendell got Sojo on that foul pop-up after he intentionally walked O'Neill. All he had to do was get Vizcaino."

The New York Mets advocate had made an excellent point. "Too many weapons on the pinstripe machine, Sully my boy. Nobody scares me in the Mets lineup except for your sole *paison*. Piazza is a great hitter."

The entire family then gathered in the living room to watch the second game of the fall classic. After eight innings, Tony's World Series wager, the Yankees winning in six games or less, was looking prophetic. Roger Clemens was masterful for the Yankees, allowing no runs and two hits. The right hander, destined for the Hall of Fame, walked none and struck out nine. The boys from the Bronx led the contingent from Queens 6–0.

Teresa Calabrese announced she was going to bed, and Maria made her way to the second floor of the house; the review of an assignment she would distribute to her English class the following day required her attention.

Hold on there, Teresa and Maria. Don't count your chickens. Do you remember the Yogi Berra refrain? "It ain't over till it's over." Perhaps their departure was premature.

Yankees skipper Joe Torre decided that Roger Clemens didn't need to further tax his right arm.

"Why is he taking Clemens out, Uncle Tony?"

Tommy Sullivan, a young baseball star on the travel team coached by his uncle, was not in agreement with the substitution made by the Yankees manager.

"All these pitchers are babied nowadays, what can I tell you? I've seen Clemens throw over 140 pitches against us when he was on the Red Sox."

Johnny Sullivan demonstrated his knowledge of baseball facts.

"Al Leiter was on the Yankees when he came up, Tommy. Their manager at the time, Dallas Green, once left Al in for 162 pitches. Some speculate that it may have led to his arm trouble as a young pitcher."

"Good memory, Sully."

Tony's response to his brother-in-law was further discussed, although briefly. The elder Sullivan had something to applaud about, as a Piazza blast into the left-field seats cut the lead to 6–2.

A third straight hit had Torre scurrying to the mound. The intention of his right-hand motion toward the bull pen was clear to all Yankees fans. It was Mariano Rivera time.

Five batters later, surprised supporters of the team seeking its third straight championship witnessed Rivera yielding a three-run home run. The scoreboard now read, Yankees, 6; Mets, 5.

In his high school and college years, Tony was known to utter profanities more than just occasionally. The exception, at least usually, was when he was within earshot of his mother.

Since his ordination, Father Tony had learned to abstain from profanity altogether.

But then, nobody's perfect, not even a priest.

"You gotta be f'n shittin' me, Mariano!" The priest was immediately apologetic. "Oh my God, sorry, kids. That was totally inappropriate, please forgive me."

Minutes later, the relief on the faces of the twins and Father Tony pervaded the Calabrese household. Rivera struck out the final batter, and the one-run Yankees lead was preserved.

To Tony's delight, his niece, Tammy, the unequivocal theatrical member of the family, mimicked the John Sterling radio call after a Yankees victory. She playfully got into her dad's face.

"The Yankees win...Theeeeeee Yankees win!"

Johnny was not enthralled with the actions of his daughter.

He just shook his head in a disgruntled manner. "All you Yankees fans are spoiled."

5

The day following the Yankees game 2 victory, Tony was continually inquiring about whether Beverly Thomas had called to make an appointment with him. The rectory administrative staff did not give him the response he had hoped for.

As he watched the New York Jets defeat the Miami Dolphins 40–37 that evening, Father Tony fretted that Beverly hadn't called. He briefly thought of discussing her revelation of the wife and child beatings with Johnny, but the realization that his priestly vow to adhere to the Seal of Confession prevented any such disclosure to a law enforcement official.

He decided on making a phone call.

"Father Carlos, it's me, Tony, I need to talk to you."

Father Anthony Calabrese always referred to his mentor as Father Carlos; this, despite the fact that priests rarely referred to one another using *father* before their first names. Tony, who had known Father Carlos since he was a young teenager, did it out of respect. They agreed to meet the following afternoon for lunch.

Father Carlos remained a mentor and confidant to the priest some fifteen years his junior. He was cognizant of the reason for the conversation. He handed Father Tony a pamphlet on the Catholic Church teachings regarding the Seal of Confession. "Read this thoroughly. I think it will guide you in your decision making. Now tell me, Anthony, did you agree with Torre taking out Clemens the other night?"

6

Three days later, Mets manager Bobby Valentine shook the hand of his Yankees counterpart; the New York Yankees were the 2000 World Series champions.

Tony spoke with his mother on the phone. "What do you think, Mom? Not only would Dad have loved the outcome but both managers were Italian."

The New York newspapers were subjugated with articles about the teams. The Yankees fans had the history, but the Mets fans remained steadfast in their recollections of 1969 and 1986.

Game 3: Mets, 4; Yankees, 2

The first game at Shea Stadium put a smile on Bobby Valentine and Mets lover faces.

Johnny Sullivan had finally earned bragging rights.
"Father Tony, its Sully. That's one."
"Be thankful you won't be swept."

Game 4: Yankees, 3; Mets, 2

Derek Jeter led off the game with a home run, and the Yankees survived another Piazza round-tripper. Rivera recorded his fifth save of the postseason.

"Get ready, Sully, there will be weeping at Shea Stadium tomorrow."

Game 5: Yankees, 4; Mets, 2

The Yankees, often considered by sports experts to be the greatest team in professional sports history, had added to their astonishing record of World Series victories. Number

26 was special, reminiscent of the Subway Series played in 1956 versus the Brooklyn Dodgers.

Maria Sullivan was ecstatic with the choice of the sportswriters for World Series MVP—Derek Jeter. The Yankees shortstop led the team with a batting average of .409.

Father Tony's delight regarding his baseball team did not diminish his angst regarding his priestly responsibilities.

"Dear Lord, please give me the wisdom to make things right for Beverly Thomas."

Chapter III

Seal of Confession

1

The Yankees had provided Tony with an additional $1,180 in winnings for the Christmas present he planned for the family. He realized that it might be wise to clue in everyone regarding his surprise: five nights on the Royal Caribbean during the Christmas holidays—destination, Bermuda. He was confident that his good friend from college, a baseball teammate, Willie "Mays" Jackson, now an executive at the cruise line, would get him a great deal.

Thoughts of the trip quickly vanished as he opened the pamphlet he received from Father Carlos.

His reading was thorough. Although the seal was integral to his priesthood education, it just wasn't an issue he had ever dwelled on.

Several statements hit him like a Mike Tyson left hook.

"The sacramental seal is inviolable."

"It is a crime for a confessor in any way to betray a penitent by word or in any other manner or for any reason."

"A priest cannot break the seal to save his own life, to protect his good name, to refute a false accusation, to save the life of another, or to aid the course of justice, such as reporting a crime." "A priest cannot reveal the contents of a confession whether directly, by repeating the substance of what has been said, or indirectly, by some sign, suggestion, or action."

Tony had forgotten the severity of his restrictions regarding the disclosure of any statement made by a penitent.

The review finally provided him with a potential solution to his dilemma. It confirmed to him that asking Beverly Thomas to meet with him was the correct course of action.

"A priest may ask the penitent for a release from the sacramental seal to discuss the confession with the person himself or others. If the penitent wants to discuss the subject matter of a previous confession in a counseling session or in

a conversation with the same priest, that priest will need the permission of the penitent to do so."

Then another alternative.

"If a priest needs guidance from a more experienced confessor to deal with a difficult case of conscience, he first must ask the permission of the penitent to discuss the matter. Even in this, the priest must keep the identity of the person secret."

He then examined the consequences of violating the vow. *"A confessor who directly violates the Seal of Confession incurs an automatic excommunication reserved to the Apostolic see; if he does so indirectly, he is to be punished in accord with the seriousness of the offense."*

It was apparent to him that meeting with Beverly was the best alternative.

2

Father Tony heard confessions as usual on Saturday afternoon. He was hoping to hear the voice of Beverly Thomas, and just before the expiration of the scheduled allocated time for penitents to cleanse their souls, he got his wish.

"Bless me, Father, for I have sinned. It's me, Beverly Thomas. I need your help, Father Tony. My husband wants to make things right. He admits that he has a drinking problem. Do you think that he and I can come in together to see you?"

"That's great to hear, Mrs. Thomas, I am available whenever you need me."

"Please, call me Beverly, Father."

Father Tony attentively listened to her plea for help. Then, the thankful confessor received a release from Beverly to discuss her situation, including anything she had revealed the previous week. His dilemma was resolved; he would not be restricted by the Seal of Confession. Now, if he felt it necessary, he could even solicit input from his mentor, Father Carlos. Father Tony was further pleased that he was acting in accordance with his priestly responsibility when a 9:30 a.m. appointment was scheduled on Monday for Beverly and her husband.

The cleric wondered how the issue of not divulging a penitent's private disclosure hadn't surfaced in the past. *Beautiful,* he thought to himself. *Now I can concentrate on the NFL games for tomorrow.* He left the confessional and sought to find his friend George.

In the back of the church, his childhood buddy awaited Tony's arrival.

"Hey, George, I hope you took my advice and went with the boys from the Bronx in the Series."

"I wish, Tony. I laid off."

"Well, you can make up for it this week, my old friend. I have a lock for you."

Father Tony then provided George with the wisdom of his weekly wagers.

"Give me a parlay for $150. I like Kerry Collins to have a big week against the Eagles, so you can give me the Giants laying three and a half. The second half of the winning duo is the Rams, minus 7, versus San Francisco."

"You got it, Tony. Here's the $1,180 you won on your Yankees World Series bets. Between the NFL and the Yankees, you are on quite a roll."

Reading the *New York Daily News* on Monday morning before his scheduled meeting with Beverly Thomas and her husband, Father Tony focused on the fact that the Giants' 24–7 triumph over the Philadelphia Eagles had disparate quarterback performances, Kerry Collins of the Giants clearly outplaying Donovan McNabb of the Eagles.

The 34–24 Rams victory over the 49ers, with Los Angeles scoring the last seventeen points of the contest, completed his winning parlay bet.

"That will cover the cost of a stretch limo for pickup to and return home from the cruise. I'm sure Tammy and Tommy will get a kick out of that."

At nine twenty-five, Father Tony was apprised that Mr. and Mrs. Thomas had arrived.

Three quarters of an hour later, the priest was amazed at the resolve of Jerry Thomas to seek help with his addiction. It certainly was an excellent beginning, he thought.

The priest provided the couple with information regarding a friend of his at Alcoholics Anonymous, and Jerry agreed to attend a meeting as soon as the following evening.

Beverly kissed him on the cheek as the couple departed. "Thank you, Father Tony."

Jerry seconded the thank-you.

"I had heard good things about you from my wife and son, Father. You listened to me without judgment. I appreciate your intercession. I don't want to lose my family."

"Listen, Jerry, you have a long road ahead. Please keep me updated regarding your progress and come in to see me whenever you feel the need."

After the couple departed, Tony was content; later that day, his spirits skyrocketed further.

Jackpot! Willie "Mays" Jackson had come through big time. After Tony had confirmed with his mom and sister that the five-day cruise would commence on the day after Christmas, a Tuesday, the itinerary was set. The Calabrese family would depart on the *Princess Voyager* at 3:00 p.m. and then ultimately disembark early on the following Sunday morning. Willie then went to work on a special deal for his college friend and baseball teammate.

The results were as astonishing as his good buddy's remarkable catches while playing center field for Manhattan College. Several of his eye-catching baseball pilfers were reminiscent of the ultimate grab of his namesake, Willie Mays, the greatest catch in World Series history with an over-the- shoulder grab of a Vic Wertz drive in the 1954 fall classic.

The phone call from the guy Tony described as the "best all-around ballplayer he ever stepped on the diamond with" was like music to his ears.

"I got you three rooms with balconies. You also will be entitled to the three-meal plan, unlimited liquor, and all refreshments [soda, bottled water, snacks, etc.] while you're on board. This is not a typical package, Tony. Your family has an exclusive deal. All you need to do is to take care of the tips while on the ship. Of course, you will be on your own in Bermuda after you dock. Oh, I forgot, your mom, sister, and niece are entitled to what we call the Royal Spa Experience."

Tony was cognizant of the fact that the price Willie quoted was less than half of the true cost.

"Thanks, Willie, you're the best. Say hello to Amanda [Willie's wife] and the kids for me."

Tony had one more conversation that day. Father Carlos was thanked for his assistance. Tony also queried his mentor about his experiences as a confessor.

"How many times did you find that it was necessary to maintain secrecy relative to a confession you heard?"

"Three, and I still can't talk about one of them. I am sure that you will be faced with future disclosures that will test your resolve. It comes with the territory, Anthony."

3

Father Tony arrived at 7:00 p.m. He had voted for Al Gore earlier in the day and now sat at the dining room table with his mother, sister, brother-in-law, niece, and nephew.

"I wish Bill Bradley had gotten the democratic nomination, he has a much better jump shot than Gore. In any event, I couldn't see myself voting for George W. I did vote for his father, though."

Johnny Sullivan rebutted his wife's brother. "I believe the time for the Dems is over. No way was I voting for the guy who served under Clinton."

The females of the Calabrese household were also split in their presidency voting allegiance. Teresa Calabrese, a longtime Democrat, concurred with her son-in-law and surprisingly voted for the former governor of Texas, while Maria Sullivan sided with her brother.

As the group watched the early election returns later that evening, it became apparent that the country's conundrum in choosing the forty-third president of the United States was equally perplexing. The State of Florida, initially a TV projection in blue, was switched to undecided, and by the time Father Tony headed back to his room at the rectory, no successor to Bill Clinton had been declared.

4

Thanksgiving Day. Tony arose that morning with thoughts of the banquet that his mom and sister were preparing. Of course, there would be a turkey, a twenty-two-pound Butterball. Supplementing the bird would be typical American household fixin's: sweet potatoes, mashed potatoes, string beans, bread stuffing, and cranberry sauce. Tony had been informed that the Calabrese family tradition of a first course inclusive of lasagna with meatballs and braciola would not be forgotten. Maria Sullivan would also add a second stuffing, made with sausage and rice.

The gathering would embrace his brother-in-law's family; Johnny was appreciative of the invite of his mom, dad, and sister. The latter, now divorced, would bring along her daughter and son.

Tony arrived at noon. "Hey, Mom, I'll help set the table, and then my butt will be in my favorite chair. I don't want to miss any football."

At 3:00 p.m., after appetizers were enjoyed during the early stages of the Detroit Lions drubbing of the New England Patriots, the sit-down dinner commenced. Father Tony was only slightly miffed that the Lions had halted his highly profitable betting winning streak.

"Hopefully the Vikings will get me even against the Cowboys in game 2."

Father Tony was happy to offer the dinner blessing, a customary occurrence at all family gatherings. The Thanksgiving prayer was even more special to the Calabrese clan, and the sentiments were shared by the Sullivans.

The principle topic of conversation at the table was one that often caused consternation at such assemblies. Fortunately, the discussion was civil, albeit contrasting in thought. The apparent election of George W. Bush, despite his opponent garnering more votes nationwide and the turmoil in Florida regarding disputed ballots, was argued vigorously but respectfully.

"Hanging chads my ass—oh, sorry, everyone." Johnny Sullivan was not an advocate of those who felt that the Florida vote should be in question but wanted to soften his language in front of the kids.

His wife shook her head and added, "Bush didn't even win the popular vote. Gore had over five hundred thousand ballots cast for him. He should be president, not Bush."

"Yeah, Mom, but as my history teacher pointed out, that is not how we elect our president. Furthermore, he didn't even win his home state."

Tommy Sullivan supported Tammy's observation. "I agree with that, sis. If you can't win the state you represented in the Senate, you don't deserve to be president."

"See there, Maria, our kids make a lot of sense. It's even worse when you realize that his father was also a senator from Tennessee."

"To tell you the truth, the more I think about it, I was not really enamored with either candidate. I am starting to believe that I should have voted for Ralph Nader" was Tony's jibe. "Enough talk regarding politics though. How would you like to hear about the room arrangements for our cruise?"

Father Tony then announced the stateroom assignments for the voyage to Bermuda aboard the Royal Caribbean. His mother would share a room with her granddaughter, Tony would double up with his nephew, and the likely pairing of his sister and brother-in-law completed the trifecta.

Tony's mom went overboard praising her son's thoughtfulness and generosity regarding the planned after-Christmas-Day cruise.

"Thank you, Mother dear, but it's really not that big of a deal."

Maria immediately sought to reinforce her mom's observation. "Your mother is absolutely right on, Tony. Just hush up and take the compliments. This trip is just so considerate of you. Johnny and I don't know how we will ever repay you."

"Repay me? My family is the most important aspect of my life. Don't you ever think that there is any need to do anything for me except to have a good time."

Tammy got up and hugged her uncle. "It will be the best Christmas present ever, the best."

This view was seconded by her twin, who added a quip he felt was clever. "Uncle Tony, thanks a lot. Although a seven-day cruise would have been better."

As everyone except for his mother, Maria, laughed at Tommy's obvious attempt to inject a little humor into the conversation, his uncle responded, "You just lost your starting center field position on the travel team."

Tony fully appreciated the adulation regarding his planned family Christmas present, and the afternoon meal was truly one to be thankful for. The distraction of sitting across from Johnny's sister posed only a minor problem. She was an attractive and shapely redhead. Her questioning of whether the pope would ever allow a priest to marry was seemingly directed at him.

"Are you testing me again, Lord?" he said to himself.

"Hey, Sully, how about an after-dinner drink? Is anyone else up for a little Sambuca?"

Chapter IV

Royal Caribbean

1

Father Tony's reputation in the parish as a priest who was there for his parishioners was further enhanced when word of his intervention in the Thomas family crisis surfaced. The plaudits of Beverly Thomas to her friends, Bobby's comments to his baseball teammates and school classmates, and perhaps most importantly the praise of Jerry Thomas in a letter addressed to the St. John the Baptist pastor all contributed to this augmentation.

Soon thereafter, Johnny, upon receiving his brother-in-law's permission, put in a recommendation for Tony to become one of the volunteer NYPD chaplains.

"There are plenty of guys who could benefit from your down-to-earth approach, and you are a lot younger than most of the chaplains I've seen."

An unexpected bonus was the invitation of Jerry Thomas to be his guest (two tickets in the twenty-sixth row from field level on the forty-yard line) at the New York Giants game versus the Pittsburgh Steelers on December 10 at the Meadowlands. He and his nephew, Tommy, would join Jerry and his son, Bobby.

December 10, 2000

Two and a half hours of tailgating in the Meadowlands parking lot had the foursome in prime spirits to see if the Giants could add to their 9–4 record and stay ahead of the Eagles for the NFC East lead.

The two boys were truly into the game, and each was particularly enamored with the Giants' 13–3 lead after the initial thirty minutes.

As the boys went for sodas, Jerry and Tony conversed. "Father, if I were the jealous type and didn't trust you, I'd be fearful that you and my wife would be an item. She is extremely fond of you, and sometimes I just don't know what to make of her constant praising of you."

Tony was transiently at a loss for words.

"Your wife is a parishioner and a good friend, Jerry. That's as far as it goes."

The Giants prevailed 30–10. Tony was delighted that he had bet on the New York team laying three and a half points. Yet he had difficulty getting the comment of his host out of his mind. He had to admit, at least to himself, that Beverly posed a real temptation. Yet a married woman never had him in a quandary. He remained confident that his vow of celibacy would not be compromised.

On the drive home, the boys were touting a Super Bowl appearance for the Giants. Jerry was excited about the victory; Tony was thankful to his host but wondered if Jerry believed his "parishioner and good friend" comment.

2

Tony's mom, assisted by Maria, prepared a Christmas Eve feast of seafood specialties for family and friends consisting of fourteen individuals. Father Tony left earlier than usual with the responsibility of serving the midnight Mass.

Christmas Day was relatively quiet. The thoughts of Tony's loved ones were focused on the cruise, which would depart the next day. There was only one eventful moment: Johnny's identification of an attempted armed robbery of a liquor store in Sheepshead Bay, Brooklyn.

"I know the cop who shot and killed the perps, two high school seniors. There were several peculiarities about the incident. The case is being investigated by my office."

Maria was not pleased with her husband. She was fearful that discussion of a liquor store murder would bring back bad memories for her brother.

"Enough about work, Johnny, talk about the trip."

3

Six smiling and exuberant inaugural cruise goers embarked the *Princess Voyager* at 1:30 p.m. on Tuesday, December 26. The ship set sail an hour and a half later. Bon voyage.

The schedule called for sailing until early Thursday morning, docking in Bermuda until late Friday afternoon, and then culminating with the return to New York and disembarking on Sunday morning, the last day of the twentieth century.

Prior to getting established in their staterooms, all were in amazement of the expanse of the vessel.

Teresa Calabrese confided in her daughter and son, "This is like its own city. I wish your father had the opportunity to take this cruise with us."

Maria blew a kiss skyward. "Dad would be in his glory—food, drink, entertainment, and family. Keep us safe, Dad."

Tommy had a comment about how his uncle would save them if there were a problem.

"I saw the *Poseidon Adventure* last week. There was a priest on board who lead several passengers to safety after the boat was submerged. We have Uncle Tony."

"First of all, my alleged intelligent son, it's called a ship, not a boat. Secondly," added a chortling Johnny, "I guess they could have used a priest on the *Titanic*."

"I would have been fine with the fact of just having Leonardo DiCaprio around" was the retort of Maria.

Tammy entered the fray with a comment on the lead actor in the 1997 film, "Yeah, Mom, you're right, he is cute."

Just prior to the request of his mother to change the subject, Father Tony was sentimental as he offered a final thought at the recollection of the *Poseidon Adventure*. He identified how Gene Hackman, who portrayed the priest, also starred as the high school basketball coach in Angela's favorite sports movie, *Hoosiers*.

"That was the last movie we ever saw together."

"Angela was a fantastic basketball player. It doesn't surprise me that *Hoosiers* was her favorite," said Maria.

Upon their arrival at the staterooms, there was a pleasant surprise; the rooms were contiguous. Tony did not realize that Willie was able to accomplish this arrangement. It made for a special family setting when all were able to converse when outside on their respective fifty-four-square-foot verandas.

The interiors were spacious enough, just under two hundred square feet, with bath, queen-size bed, sitting area with a thirty- six-inch TV, minibar, and private safe.

Tommy and Tammy separated from the four adults prior to the evening dinner under the instruction of meeting at the entrance to the main dining hall at five minutes to seven. Their glee was paramount upon finding a basketball court; a miniature golf course; a colossal game room; a rock climbing wall; several pools, one that had a sign for 10:00 a.m. pool volleyball the following morning; and most importantly, a teen nightclub.

Tony's mom, sister, brother-in-law, and he all agreed that a cocktail before dinner was in order. One flight up the stairway from their current living quarters on the ninth level led to the Blarney Pub, a suggestion of Johnny Sullivan.

Each presented a card as the waitress approached, the entitlement of unlimited liquid refreshments, including alcoholic beverages. Johnny and Tony each ordered a pint of Guinness, while the ladies decided on Pinot Grigio.

A first swallow of his dark hops had Johnny smiling. "These cards are unbelievable, Tony. Thanks."

"You can thank my friend Willie for that, Sully. He had that perk included with our package."

The New York law enforcement employee grinned as he then inquired, "I wonder who they will put with us for dinner services?"

"We'll soon find out," responded his wife.

The main dining hall was another level up. Everyone was accounted for, so the six entered to find their assigned table, number 56.

Tony was pleased with the assigned table digits, which corresponded to the jersey of the football player favored by both he and his departed girlfriend, New York Giants linebacker Lawrence Taylor.

"LT was simply the best. Angela and I only agreed on one sports team, the Giants. Number 56 was her favorite player.

"Your father liked the Giants also. His favorite player was Andy Robustelli."

"I wonder why, Ma," Maria responded with the recognition of the importance of the Italian heritage to her father.

Then an interruption. "Is this table 56?"

Teresa Calabrese answered the dapper gentleman speaker. She judged his age to be similar to her own. "You've come to the right place, I'm Teresa." She then introduced the rest of the family.

"Hi, Teresa, my name is Paul. This is my daughter, Donna, and my grandchildren, Scott and Becky."

Soon there were ten smiling faces, only one of which was a little uncomfortable. Temptation had surfaced again, this time finding its way to the seat next to him. He guessed that Donna was in her midthirties. She was tall, exceedingly attractive, and a brunette with brown eyes; Angela immediately entered his mind.

Johnny, to the left of Tony, nudged the thigh of his brother-in-law and whispered, "Do you need to switch seats?"

Teresa Calabrese soon learned Paul was a widower, a semiretired advertising executive, and was sixty-six years old. He looked much younger, still retaining his dark hair, with gray evident only above his sideburns and ears.

Scott and Becky, fourteen and thirteen respectively, provided instant companionship for the twins.

Tony's conversation with the newly arrived eye-catching female revealed that she was a widow, her husband passing two years prior. Upon learning of her loss and offering his sincere condolences, the priest thought of identifying his own travails but withheld such information.

At the culmination of the dinner, the four teens scurried off to check out the club tailored for their age group; the others found their way to the Sapphire Lounge for an after-dinner drink.

Father Tony deliberated briefly on the questioning of Paul and Donna regarding his inspiration of becoming a Catholic priest and then excused himself and headed for the casino. He was anxious to observe what the high stakes on the seas offered and also saw the need to distance himself from the enticement of his recent female acquaintance.

His evening prayers included a request to repress lustful thoughts regarding the eye-catching woman he had met that evening.

4

Teresa Calabrese had suggested an 8:00 a.m. breakfast time for her family. All gathered outside their staterooms at five minutes before the hour and then departed for the morning cuisine.

The twins were effusive of their new friends from Long Island and had planned to meet at 10:00 a.m. for pool volleyball.

Teresa Calabrese tried to remain composed, but her fondness for Paul Bathgate was apparent to her daughter.

"Paul seems like a real nice guy, Mom. How long ago did he lose his wife?"

"Five years ago, after being married for thirty-three years."

Maria Sullivan continued, "Donna was highly complimentary of you, Tony. She indicated that it was unfortunate her parish priests were not as approachable as you are."

"Hello there, fellow members of dinner table 56."

Taking their seats at the adjacent unassigned breakfast table were Paul, Donna, Scott, and Becky.

"Why don't we ask if we can put these tables together?"

Johnny Sullivan's suggestion was happily accepted by almost everyone. Father Tony was apprehensive. The recollection of his initial meeting with the woman who reminded him of Angela was cause for a restless night's sleep.

The morning mealtime discussion was primarily focused on the planned events for the day. The four teens would commence their first full cruise day playing water volleyball.

Maria and Johnny were anxious to walk off the breakfast they were each enjoying and then change into bathing suits and lounge by the pool.

Teresa beamed at Paul's suggestion to join her in browsing at the high-end trunk shows. She was secretly interested in buying watches for her entire family.

Thankfully, Donna was inclined to initiate the reading of the newest James Patterson novel from the Alex Cross series, *Pop Goes the Weasel*, leaving Father Tony to fend for himself, or so he thought. An hour after the morning meal, he found himself walking by her as she read on a poolside lounge chair.

"Hi, Donna. Sorry, I probably should be addressing you by your surname, what is it, by the way?"

"Well, Father, I was brought up as a Bathgate and then took on my husband's name, Banks. I still go by Donna Banks, but I would prefer that you just call me Donna."

"That's fine. I'll leave you to get caught up with the exploits of Alex Cross."

"No, Father, please stay. I would like to ask you a few questions about my faith in God. I have had difficulty since my husband died."

An affirmative nod from Father Anthony Calabrese had Donna rising to adjust her sitting apparatus, such that it was immediately adjacent to where the priest had reclined.

Father Tony was awestruck by the hourglass shape of the woman he had met the previous evening. She stood at five feet, nine and a half inches and weighed 145 pounds. She reminded him of Angela, who was slightly taller but less endowed than the captivating brunette. He valiantly endeavored to listen to Donna without succumbing to visual contact below the level of her eyes. The top to her two-piece bathing suit revealed cleavage, which presented a distraction to his mission of offering assistance. A half an hour later, there was a comforting identification that was accompanied by a gleaming smile.

"You have a wonderful way about you, Father. I feel that I can tell you anything."

Tony had no such deliberations. *There is no way that I can tell her what I am thinking.*

The discourse continued for another twenty-five minutes before Tony made an excuse to abscond. He had combated feelings of not remaining chaste in the past, but the realization that this temptation was all too manifest scared him.

Immediately following the priest's departure, the engrossing female was approached for the third time since she had commenced her reading of the Patterson mystery.

The current applicant in the pickup artist role was over ten years her junior and displayed abs that would have impressed the vast majority of women.

"If I told you that you had a beautiful body, would you hold it against me?"

The rebuttal of the paralegal who had graduated from St. John's University and now was employed part-time at the law firm of Milano, Simon, and McCarthy in Garden City, Long Island, was without hesitation. Getting hit on was not an unusual occurrence for her, evidenced by her quick wit.

"If I said that I wanted to check out your ass, would you turn around and walk away?"

The abrupt dismissal afforded the lovely Ms. Banks to concentrate—no, not on Alex Cross but, rather, on the Catholic cleric whom she found so intriguing.

Tony meandered around the ship without focus, finally finding Maria and Johnny playing miniature golf a little before noon. His sister advised him that they were meeting his mother at one thirty.

"At the Burger Barn, Tony. We can get something light to hold us over until dinner. Afterward, Mom, Tammy, and I are going for our Royal Spa Experience. That was so thoughtful of you to include that amenity."

The Catholic priest left his sibling and found a lounge that he felt was obscure.

"My father always taught me never to have a drink in the morning. It's 12:01 p.m., bartender. Let me have a Grey Goose martini on the rocks with olives. Make it a little dirty."

5

You would have thought that the Calabrese and Bathgate families had known each other for years. The Wednesday evening dinner was jovial; even Tony appeared to be at ease.

"My dad followed hockey and was a Ranger fan. Probably because they had a defenseman of Italian descent named—"

"Fontinato," Paul interrupted the priest.

Tony was impressed. "Are you a Ranger fan?"

"Of course, Father. With a name like Bathgate, what did you expect? Andy Bathgate was my favorite player."

"Fontinato and Bathgate were before my time, Paul, but I have been a Ranger fan all my life. Thank God we won the Cup in '94."

Paul was gleeful. "One of my biggest thrills was watching Messier raise the Stanley Cup at the Garden. I was with my son- in-law, may he rest in peace."

The sports discussion eventually shifted to favorite TV shows.

Maria had a story about one of her tenth-grade students who had written a report on the TV show *Seinfeld*.

"She was quite astute in her analysis of the show. I found it fascinating how she discussed discrepancies in the actions of George and Kramer, suggesting that perhaps the writers of the TV series from season to season had varying views on those characters. Her examples included two extremes of George's behavior. On the one hand, performing the ultrabrave act of a supposed marine biologist who enters the ocean to remove a golf ball that had inhibited the breathing of a beached whale, while on the other, being the first person to exit a smoke-filled room of children enjoying the performance of a clown at the birthday party of his girlfriend's son and knocking down her grandmother, yelling 'Fire' as he hastily left the others to fend for themselves."

Donna seconded the thought process of Maria's student.

"What about Kramer? I remember the episode where Jerry, Elaine, and George marvel at his description of taking the wheel of a driverless bus with one hand while fending off a thug with the other. Then, in contrary fashion, allowing two effeminate guys to take Elaine's armoire as he is supposed to be on watch, protecting her newly purchased piece of furniture."

Johnny chimed in. "The armoire was the 'Soup Nazi' episode. I think that was the best show of them all. To make up for his failure in watching the armoire, Kramer gets the soup Nazi to give up his armoire, and Elaine finds all his soup recipes in it." "I watch the reruns with Johnny all the time now," added Maria Sullivan. "Too bad 1999 was the last year."

"Mom lets us watch once in a while," interjected Tammy. "Yeah," added her twin, "unless she feels the content is too sexual. She threw us out of the room when we were watching the episode about the contest Jerry, Elaine, George, and Kramer had." "Oh, I know which one you are talking about, Tommy," said his new friend Scott.

"You be quiet, you." Donna requested that a different episode other than the risqué network depiction of the bet regarding abstinence from self-gratification be discussed.

Teresa Calabrese put in her two cents. "My favorite episode was 'Yada Yada.'"

Paul Bathgate cast his vote for the "Chinese Restaurant."

"When the owner finally has a table ready for Jerry and his friends and screams out 'Seinfeld, four!' after they feel that waiting any longer would be futile and have left, I laughed hysterically."

"Any episode with Newman always cracks me up."

The priest was comfortable with the down-to-earth remark that he was a big fan of the show. He was thankful that his involvement regarding a discussion of the "Contest" episode and the potential for the topic of masturbation to surface was not required.

For the rest of the cruise, Father Tony endeavored to avoid being alone with Donna. He realized that the inducement of the riveting lass would be minimized if he could just prevent one-on-one encounters. He succeeded until the evening prior to their final disembarking.

6

While the four teenagers hurried off to their age-appropriate nightclub, the adults decided to attend the 9:00 p.m. Royal Caribbean production of *A Chorus Line*, a suggestion of Maria Sullivan.

The pamphlet handout identified that the musical sensation, which first opened in 1975, was the longest-running show in Broadway history when it closed in 1990.

Maria, an avid Broadway attendee, usually with her girlfriends, noted that she believed *Cats* had surpassed that mark a few years ago.

"I saw both shows on Broadway and enjoyed them immensely. If I had to pick one, it would be the show we are about to see. I love the song 'What I Did for Love.'"

After the performance, everyone agreed with Maria's preassessment and was supported by the accolades of several hundred cruise goers in the Royal Caribbean Theater. The standing ovation upon the culmination of the iconic Broadway show was a testament to this view.

Paul Bathgate complimented Maria. "You certainly know your Broadway shows, Maria."

"Yes, she does," proclaimed a proud mother. "I've gone into Manhattan with her for several matinees."

"So I guess you must be a Broadway fan also, Teresa. I would love to take you sometime."

"That would be wonderful, Paul."

Father Tony was pleased that his mother had met someone whose company she enjoyed. For several years he and his sister had often encouraged her to date. He felt it was a good opportunity to extend the evening.

"How about a nightcap, everybody?"

To his chagrin, the suggestion was heeded by only one person.

"I would love to, Father," responded Donna.

During the ensuing two hours, the attraction between the priest and Donna Banks became increasingly evident. Their respective life stories were shared.

Donna was tearful as she revealed that her husband, a construction supervisor for an electrical contractor, was killed while assisting an elderly couple whose car had broken down on the Long Island Expressway. "Richie was always there to help others."

The identification of the priest with regard to the bereavement support group he often conducted to assist those struggling with the loss of a loved one was of interest to Donna. "Please let me know when you are having your next meeting, Father, I would like to attend."

Tony was very forthcoming regarding the tragic loss of Angela Santino and the further emotional loss of his dad.

"I still blame myself for letting Angela enter the liquor store without me. Then I think about procrastinating giving her an engagement ring. She was the best thing that ever happened to me."

"You shouldn't blame yourself, Father. I believe in my heart that she prays for you to forgive yourself."

Donna was then in tears when the priest described a second major travail of his prepriesthood life: the death of his father. He sorrowfully described the time he had taken Nick Calabrese to Sloan Kettering Hospital a month after the diagnosis of pancreatic cancer.

"The doctor asked him, 'Have you thought about dying?' I knew then there was no hope."

The correlation between Tony, thirty-six, and Donna, who had just recently reached the midpoint of her thirties, were twofold; an emotional bond complimented the physical magnetism, which was unmistakable, commencing on the evening of their initial encounter. Father Tony realized that the inducement of being in the company of this beautiful and compassionate woman was beyond his facility to control. A polite suggestion that he shepherd the widowed mother of two to her stateroom ensued.

"Let me escort you back to your room. The ship will be docking early in the morning."

Father Tony thought about holding her hand on the saunter to her cruise quarters but opted for a more apposite taking of her arm under his. The walk seemed endless to the cleric; the conversation, guarded.

"Thank you for keeping me company, Father. Your sincerity is very evident. There is no phoniness in your makeup. I wish I were able to speak with you after Richie was killed."

"It was my pleasure, Donna. I hope that I was of some help and comfort to you. You certainly were a very good listener regarding my trials and tribulations. I certainly opened up to you, and I am so thankful to have met you."

The priest then gallantly ventured to keep his posture on a lower keel. The allure of the woman who aroused true feelings in him that were absent since St. Patrick's Day of 1987 proved this to be an insurmountable endeavor, particularly after she gently kissed him on his lips as the two reached her cruise quarters.

The buss triggered a further mutual reaction. Father Tony recalled the phrase "Speaking in tongues." There was little, if any, speaking but certainly no lack of tongues. Tony's hands soon firmly groped her buttocks; his penis pressed up against her. Donna was fully responsive to his every action.

"Mom, is that you?"

Thankfully for Father Tony, the voice of Donna's daughter, Becky, was heard from inside the stateroom.

7

The limousine-ride home was fraught with stories. Everyone contributed the recollection of a cruise event that was particularly singular, save for the person responsible for making the excursion possible.

"The teen nightclub was the best. I wish we had one in Queens."

"Yeah, Tammy," added her twin brother, "but I think my favorite time on the trip was scuba diving in Bermuda. It was also great to make new friends. I'm sure you agree, Tammy." He added with a smirk, "I saw the way you looked at Scott."

"Well, you had googly eyes for Becky, so I wouldn't talk."

"All right, you two. I loved everything about it, but if I had to pick one thing, it would be looking at Johnny's expression when I made the hole in one to beat him by a stroke in miniature golf."

"Lucky shot, Maria, just lucky," added her husband. "I was impressed with the variety of lounges on the ship. Of course, my favorite was the Blarney Pub."

Teresa Calabrese was just thankful to be with her family and was coy regarding her feelings toward Paul Bathgate. "Paul is a very nice gentleman. He said he would call me."

Maria smiled. "He really likes you, Mom."

"Do you really think so? Oh, by the way, I have a surprise for everyone when we get home."

"I think I may know, Grandma. I saw you packing something you didn't want me to see."

The twins also had a surprise. It was for their uncle Tony, to thank him for his generosity. Tammy commenced the dialogue. "Tommy and I bought gifts to thank you, Father Tony. You gave us the best Christmas present ever."

"Yeah, Uncle Tony, I think you'll like what we got you. You can hang them in your room at the rectory."

"Dummy, now you've given it away," said Tammy.

Tony, usually ebullient under similar circumstances, seemed rather subdued as he thanked his niece and nephew. Johnny Sullivan noticed.

"Yo, earth to Father Tony, why so quiet? Did you go to the casino last night and leave a bundle at the blackjack table?" Johnny waited for a response from his wife's brother.

Tony feigned a smile. "Just thinking, Sully, just thinking."

8

Father Tony opened the gifts from his niece and nephew when he arrived back at the rectory. He was pleasantly surprised and very appreciative. He opted to make an immediate phone call of thanks.

The framed picture depicting the Super Bowl XXI winner Phil Simms hugging teammate Lawrence Taylor after the game was a definite keeper. Simms, the quarterback who had one of the greatest days in Super Bowl history, and Taylor, the linebacker whom both he and Angela deemed their favorite Giants and whom Tony considered the greatest defensive player of all- time, would be proudly displayed on his wall.

A second photo, portraying a jubilant group of young hockey players, brought back memories to him. He recalled watching the 1980 Olympic hockey team victory over the USSR at Lake Placid with his family.

His thoughts focused on his deceased father. "What a game, right, Dad? We were all chanting 'USA! USA!'"

Chapter V

NYPD Chaplain

1

The New Year's Eve party in the auditorium of the St. John the Baptist School was attended by close to two hundred parishioners, principally couples. Father Tony was one of the two priests who assisted the New Year's Eve committee with monitoring the event.

The alcohol was limited to wine, beer, and punch; the music, somewhat diverse, ranged from oldies to hits from the most recent decade.

Tony was not shy about strutting his stuff on the dance floor and, when prompted by one of the married mothers of his baseball travel team, wowed the attendees with his moves. He purposely refrained, however, from the many slow dance requests he received, always indicating that he had to administer to a function responsibility.

While listening to several songs such as the Billy Joel classic "Just the Way You Are," Tony recalled slow dancing with Angela; the memory of her body intertwined with his, as one, was unforgettable to him. He remained happiest when thinking about her, at least until recently. Now, although he tried not to, thoughts of another woman were prevalent.

Tony looked at the Movado watch that his mom had bought him on the cruise. It was twenty minutes until midnight. Soon the big screen in the room would depict the gleaming and familiar face of Dick Clark in Times Square, an image witnessed by millions of Americans every year since 1974. He wondered how he would react if Donna Banks were present.

2

"What do you think about the family getting a puppy?" Johnny Sullivan queried his brother-in-law.

"You know that I love dogs, but it won't be me taking care of the pooch, other than when I visit."

"Yeah, I know, but I wanted your input. I think your mom and the kids would love having a dog around, and Maria has always been a dog admirer."

"What brought this up, Sully?"

"The firehouse in the neighborhood has a Golden Retriever who had puppies. They think the father is a chocolate Labrador Retriever who went to visit once. There is one male and one female pup unspoken for. I asked if they could wait until tomorrow for a decision, and they agreed."

"I say go for it, Johnny. What is the coloring of the remaining two pups?"

"The male favors the mother's color, golden. The female took on more of the chocolate color of the father."

"Talk to your wife, Sully, let her pick. Can you take Maria down to the firehouse to check the puppies out?"

"Good idea, I'll do that. By the way, Tony, I've got good news. Your volunteer assignment as an NYPD chaplain was approved. You will be a real asset."

3

Teresa Calabrese cooked an elaborate dinner for the family that Sunday. A group that now included a female Golden Retriever / Labrador Retriever mix with chocolate coloring.

Tammy and Tommy loved the name that their grandmother had selected for the pooch.

"Seven is a real cool name, Grandma."

"Yeah, Nan, naming the puppy in honor of Mickey Mantle by using his uniform number is a great idea. Two weeks ago I saw the *Seinfeld* episode rerun where George Costanza wanted to name his first child Seven."

"Well, you two know that Mickey Mantle was my favorite player. His picture is in my bedroom. It's the one where you see my uncle Peter getting him to autograph a baseball for me. That was 1961. I still have that ball, do you want to see it?" The twins happily indicated their desire to see it, and Teresa Calabrese coalesced to the request, bringing both the autographed ball and the framed photograph. "Wow, Nan, Mickey Mantle is cute."

"He was a heartthrob of mine for sure, Tammy."

Author's note:
the photo actually
depicts my Uncle
Vin having Mickey
sign a baseball that
was autographed
for me in 1961.

The pup was getting the acclamation that Mama Calabrese typically would heap on her son. Tony didn't mind; he took his turn holding the affectionate animal, who seemingly loved everyone, superimposing her tongue with licks for all.

"OK, Seven, let's see if you are going to be a good-luck charm for the Giants. It looks as if the Ray Lewis interception for a touchdown has put away the Titans in the AFC postseason game. Switch over to the Giants pregame show, Tommy. It's time to get ready to watch Big Blue put a hurtin' on the Eagles." The football team favored by almost every household member, the Giants, was set to play their first play-off game of the season. The previous week the team had earned a bye, having won their division and finishing as the top-ranked team in the NFC.

Father Tony had bet a parlay on the Baltimore Ravens and Giants. The $100 wager had begun as planned with the Ravens winning the game outright, despite being a six-point underdog. Now his favorite team required a victory by more than four and a half points. Tony hoped to make up for his losing wager that Saturday, when the second half of his $100 parlay, the Miami Dolphins, getting nine points from the Oakland Raiders, were crushed 27–0.

The Eagles scored a touchdown with just under two minutes remaining in the Meadowlands. No worries, though; the Giants were leading 20–3 at the time, and the ten-point final margin of victory put the priest in a good mood as he playfully threw a miniature stuffed football to Seven.

His mother had another surprise as everyone enjoyed her homemade cannoli cake for desert.

It seemed the appropriate time for Teresa Calabrese to make an announcement. "Paul is coming for dinner next Sunday with Donna and her kids."

Tammy and Tommy welcomed the news. "I bet Scott and Becky will love Seven."

"They love football too. We can all watch the Giants win again."

Maria was happy for her mother. "That's great, Mom."

Father Tony refrained from commenting, contemplating how he would cope with his ensuing Donna Banks encounter.

4

The initial recipient of counseling from Father Tony, in his role as chaplain, was Patrolman Andrew "Andy" Miller. The police officer of almost four years was quite disillusioned regarding the shooting of two young armed robbers in Sheepshead Bay, Brooklyn. The officer responsible was his brother, Alex, five years his senior. The conversation commenced with a question. "My name is Andrew Miller, Father. My friends call me Andy.

Are you the priest from St. John the Baptist Parish who founded the bereavement support group there?"

"Yes, Andy, I am. Father Anthony Calabrese. Those who know me call me Father Tony."

"My mother has attended several of your sessions, Father Tony. Her twin sister had a massive heart attack and passed away last September, and she told me all about how you have enabled her to better cope with the grief. She mentioned that you had discussed your own life tragedies and that you would soon be assisting the NYPD as a volunteer chaplain. That's why I looked you up. I'd like your input on something."

"I hope that I can be of assistance to you also, Andy." "Well, Father, I am here because my mother and I are concerned about my brother, Alex. He was the officer who shot and killed two young armed robbers at a liquor store in Sheepshead Bay six weeks ago, and he expresses no feelings of remorse. He has been drinking and gambling excessively, and the only thing he cares about is his new Mustang. Maybe I shouldn't be so surprised, since he was always that way before he became a cop but had gotten a little better . . . Oh, forget about it, Father. I've said too much already."

The dialogue with Andy Miller was puzzling to the pristine chaplain. He considered his original foray with the NYPD a failure. He called his brother-in-law that evening.

"Hey, Sully, you may have recommended the wrong guy for the chaplain role."

Tony described the earlier day's discussion.

Detective Johnny Sullivan was intrigued.

"I know Andy's brother, Alex. I was beginning to tell you about him before we went on the cruise, remember? I mentioned the shooting before Maria told me to drop it."

"Oh, yeah, I do recollect that."

"The shooting incident was investigated. There were a few peculiarities, but Alex was found to have acted in accordance with police protocol, and the case was closed."

"I don't understand, Sully. What do you mean by *peculiarities*?" "Well, Alex's partner was checking on the store owner, who had been struck in the head and didn't witness the shootings, and only one of the perps had a gun. Alex said they both had guns."

5

That Saturday afternoon, during an interlude as a confessor at the penance service, Tony began thinking about how he would wager on the following day's NFC and AFC Championship games. He endeavored not to reflect on the upcoming Sunday dinner, which would require his reconnection with Donna, a subject that dominated his thoughts every night as he lay in bed after his evening prayers.

Afterward, in their customary meeting spot in the rear of the church, George noticed that his friend was not himself as the two discussed the priest's pigskin prognostications.

"Get with it, Tony. The Giants are in the NFC Championship game!"

"Just have a few things on my mind, my good friend. By the way, I have a joke for you. Actually, a series of them."

"Let's hear what you got, Tony."

"The following are several of the rules that men wished women knew. One of the fathers on my travel baseball team stopped by last week and had me laughing with them."

- Sunday sports is like the full moon or changing of the tides—just let it be.
- Anything you wear is fine. Really.
- Yes and no are perfectly acceptable answers.
- If you ask a question you don't want an answer to, expect an answer that you don't want to hear.
- Yes, peeing standing up is more difficult than doing so from point-blank range. We're bound to miss sometimes.

"Not bad, Father Tony, but you don't expect me to bring these up to Jacklyn when I get home, do you? She has a pretty good right cross."

"That's one problem I don't have."

6

Father Anthony Calabrese arrived early for the dinner that his mom had fussed over the entire week. Tony was cognizant of the fact that the kickoff for his football team was scheduled for 12:30 p.m.

"Come here, Seven. Have you been a good girl this week? Are you ready for when the company gets here? Is my mom going crazy?

"She has been keeping me sane, Anthony. I'm so nervous about today."

"Wow, Mom, something tells me that Paul is more than just a typical guest. Cooking for family and friends is usually a piece of cake for you."

The conversation distracted Father Tony from his own trepidation. He wondered how he would behave upon seeing Donna again.

"Hi, Uncle Tony, I mean, Father Tony. I bought a Giants scarf for Seven to wear for the game today."

"Only my sister would think of something like that, right, Father Tony?"

The comments from Tony's niece and nephew, whom he looked upon as if his own, put a smile on the priest's face.

"TV time, kids, where is your dad? I want your New York Jets–loving father rooting for the Giants today too."

Tony had only wagered on the Giants for the Sunday NFL play-off games. He wasn't enamored with the AFC Championship game between the Ravens and Raiders and also realized that the viewing of the game may interfere with his mom's dinner. With the Giants a surprising one-point underdog, to Tony at least, his bet was $500.

"We are at home and still getting a point, not bad. I worry about the Vikings passing game, but I love the way Kerry Collins is throwing the ball lately. His confidence is soaring."

The arrival of the Bathgate/Banks brigade at five minutes to two was greeted by Teresa Calabrese, the twins, and an excited puppy. Maria Sullivan soon followed upon completing the assignment of stirring the sauce her mother had prepared. Johnny left his chair and was heartfelt while shaking the hand of Paul Bathgate. His wife had encouraged him to be *extra nice* to the gentleman whom she felt was a perfect match for her mom.

By the time the Catholic priest made his way to participate in the welcoming committee for the foursome his family had befriended on the cruise, he was in the proper frame of mind. The Giants were dominating on the gridiron; their 24–0 lead, still minutes before halftime, had the home team crowd in a frenzy.

Father Tony placed a firm grip on the hand of Paul Bathgate and then did the same with Donna's son, Scott. He politely hugged Becky and then respectfully did likewise to the woman who had been foremost in his thoughts all week.

Teresa Calabrese was sensitive to the wishes of her son regarding the viewing of his sports teams. She had planned to serve just appetizers in the family room until the Giants game was completed. The formal sit-down at the dining room table set for ten would be upon the game's completion.

Plans changed when the score at the Meadowlands in New Jersey swelled to 34–0 by halftime.

"Do you want everyone to sit in the dining room, Ma? The Lord is looking favorably on Big Blue."

Father Tony sat at the far end of the mahogany dining room table that had been in the family since he was five years old. He was honored to take his place in the chair his father had occupied for all family dinners. Johnny sat to his left, and the person requested by his mother to sit to his right was identified.

"That is your seat, Donna, next to Father Tony."

Donna, wearing a dress considerably more conservative than one she would typically adorn, absent of any exposure of her ample breasts, glanced at Tony as he held her chair to sit.

"Thank you, Father, chivalry lives."

7

Father Tony was grateful that Donna had made the Sunday dinner experience comfortable for him, particularly since their mutual attraction had not waned in any way. At the end of the evening, the priest indicated that perhaps they could meet for lunch in the near future, identifying an Italian restaurant in eastern Queens that he believed she would enjoy. He indicated that it would be "on the Giants."

Monday morning originated a busy week at St. John the Baptist. In addition to having the responsibility for the weekday 9:00 a.m. Mass, Father Tony met with several couples who were completing their premarriage meetings during the period of the parish banns of marriage announcements. Attendance as the consoling representative of the parish at three wakes, two late morning funeral masses, the oversight of a bereavement meeting, and the need to commence preparations for the late spring/summer travel baseball team that he would once again coach further engaged his time. He was grateful to be busy; it limited his thoughts regarding Donna Banks.

On that Friday afternoon, he was somewhat apprehensive about his second session as an NYPD chaplain. His presence was anticlimactic, however; the officers he spoke with, one male and one female, were both comforted by his pleasant demeanor and ability to listen without interrupting them.

The next day, with the penance service nearly complete, Father Tony was ready to head back to his living quarters at the rectory. There would be no betting on this day; the Super Bowl between the New York Giants and Baltimore Ravens was not until the following weekend.

Could be a little boring tomorrow, he said to himself. *No football.* His thought process was then discontinued.

"Bless me, Father, for I have sinned." The voice was vaguely familiar; the penitent soon became apparent. It was police officer Andy Miller.

"It's been a few years since my last confession, Father, and I certainly have much to be repentant of."

The patrolman then rattled off a multitude of transgressions. Father Tony began to advise Andy of his penance but was disrupted.

"Father, the confessing of those sins is not the principal reason I came today. I need to reveal something that has haunted me since I was a young teenager. It involves my older brother, Alex."

The officer then described incidents involving armed robberies in the late eighties, one which involved a shooting. "I have never talked about these events before with anyone other than my mother, Father. I think my brother, Alex, may have been involved."

The next several minutes of specific revelations of the New York City cop were haunting to the Catholic priest. He tried not to be too inquisitive and to just fulfill the role of listener. The problem was the fact that one tale had similarities to an event in his own life: the fateful St. Patrick's Day evening of 1987.

"Why have you decided to reveal this in confession, Andy? It is becoming evident to me that there may be facts regarding these stories that would more appropriately be discussed with your superiors."

Andy Miller remained momentarily silent and then questioned his confessor.

"My mother mentioned to me that at one of her sessions, you spoke about the story of your girlfriend's murder. She said that it had occurred at a Bay Ridge liquor store, is that true?"

"Yes, Andy, it was almost fourteen years ago."

After a moment of silence, Andrew Miller continued, "Did the police ever arrest the killer?"

"No, the entire incident went unresolved."

The priest then confided in the penitent, blaming himself for allowing his fiancée-to-be to go into the liquor store alone. "Don't blame yourself, Father. The blame is solely on the perp who fired the gun."

"I still feel responsible, Andy."

Andrew Miller wanted to converse further about the subject but was reluctant.

"You are bound to keep this confidential, Father, right?"

"Yes, Andy."

"I may have information of importance to you. I need to talk to my mother again first."

8

The following day, family dinner gathering provided Father Tony with an opportunity to question his brother-in-law about Alex Miller. His inquiry was under the guise of being a helpful NYPD chaplain; in reality, he just wanted to learn more about the older brother of Andy Miller. He realized that his query had to be careful; the Seal of Confession once again surfaced.

"What else can you tell me about Alex Miller? I've spoken with his brother, Andy, and was thinking that perhaps I should see if I could be of assistance to him. The killing of those two teenagers has to be on his mind, right?"

The NYPD Detective first-grade, recently promoted from second-grade based on his stellar arrest performance, shook his head and replied incredulously, "The word in his precinct is that he is oblivious, almost as if the shooting had never happened. He is only concerned about the ponies, and that includes the one with wheels, his Mustang."

"Are you two talking about work? Tony, it's hard for me to believe that you are not touting our team to win the Super Bowl, and Johnny, I would have thought that you'd be giving my brother a hard time and suggesting that it is going to be the end of the line for the Giants."

Maria caused an abrupt end to the priest's investigation. "OK, sis, you're right, but the game is not until next week.

By the way, I feel that the Giants will have to play their A game to beat Baltimore. The Ravens defense, with Ray Lewis in the middle, is playing lights-out."

"What are we doing for the game, by the way?" inquired Johnny.

Teresa Calabrese smiled. "I invited Paul to come over with Donna and the kids. I hope that is all right for everyone?"

"He better be rooting for the Giants, Ma."

"Well, he is a Jets fan," responded his mother. "But Paul said he'll be pulling for the New York team, that is, when he is not concentrating on the TV commercials. He was instrumental in assisting with the development of the Budweiser ads for this year's big game."

That evening, after his litany of prayers before going to bed, two things were on his mind: Andy Miller's story and Donna. Within minutes, the focus was entirely on the woman he had become so enamored of.

Chapter VI

Father Carlos

1

Super Bowl XXXV was to be played at Raymond James Stadium in Tampa, the home field for both the NFL Tampa Bay Buccaneers and the Bulls of South Florida College. The *New York Daily News* Saturday paper was projecting game time temperatures in the high fifties, approximately twenty-five degrees warmer than the Big Apple.

Tony perused the last-minute comments of the Giants and Raven players prior to heading over to the church and taking his seat in the confessional. He noted that the point spread on the game remained unchanged from the previous day. Baltimore was a three-point favorite. He knew he would place a wager on his team but was unsure of the amount. The Ravens defense was indomitable, even hotter than the Giants offense, which was prolific in the NFC Championship game versus the Vikings. The fleeting stroll from the rectory to the enclosure he would occupy for the next two hours crystallized his philosophy on a betting quantity.

The confessions of two penitents, one of each sex, proved to be disturbing. He recognized the voice of neither. Father Tony listened to their respective revelations of spousal infidelity. As the second of the two parishioners vacated the confessional, Father Tony thought about the potential of unfaithfulness   to his priestly vow. How could he avoid succumbing to the inducement of Donna Banks?

Afterward, the discussion with George was brief. "The spread is three points, right?"

"You got it, Father Tony."

"Let the $500 from the NFC Championship game ride, George."

"I figured you for a grand."

"The Raven defense has me worried. No sense pushing it."

2

Father Tony served at the 10:00 a.m. Sunday Mass and called his mother afterward.

"What time is the company coming, Ma?"

"I told them to be here at two thirty. The kids are going to watch the movie *The Blues Brothers* before the game. Maria rented it for them and said that she and Johnny will watch it also. Paul and I are thinking about it, and I am not sure about Donna. Do you want to watch it again? I know it is one of your favorites."

"Yeah, why not. I love Jake and Elwood, and I need to tune up my Blues Brothers dancing technique. Also, it will be fun offering insights to the kids as the movie goes along. By the way, do you need help with anything? I can be there by one thirty."

"That's fine. I am just serving the food buffet style. I thought it would be easier."

"Teresa Rosa Calabrese, that is not typical of you. What is on your menu?"

"I made eggplant parmigiana, chicken cutlets, and stuffed mushrooms. I bought plenty of cold cuts and sliced cheeses and also have my homemade potato salad and coleslaw. Your sister insisted on making a large tray of baked ziti and a salad, so there will be more than enough to eat."

"I think you are ready, Ma. Do you want me to bring Italian bread from Simonetti's?"

"Good thing you asked, Anthony. I just have white and rye bread here. Can you bring a box of miniature pastries while you're at it?"

"No problem, Mother dearest. I'll get an assortment. Two dozen should do it, right?"

"Perfect."

3

Tony was pleased with the array of miniature Italian pastries available at Simonetti's bakery. A half dozen cannoli, napoleon, zeppole, and *sfogliatelle* filled the box and shared the shopping bag with four seeded loaves of Italian bread. He was greeted warmly by his mom and Seven on his arrival.

"I have a special treat for you, Seven." Tony had the cute puppy sit before rewarding her with a steak bone that one of his parishioners had given him for the pooch after the morning Mass service. The affectionate and endearing Golden-and- Labrador-Retriever mix was in her glory.

As Maria, Johnny, and the twins entered the first-floor residence of Teresa Calabrese, an excruciating sixteen-stair jaunt from the second floor of the house, Father Tony laughed as he spoke, "Good thing you didn't hit any traffic on the way down."

"Are we practicing our funny lines for the company, younger brother?

Before the cleric could respond, Maria continued, "Here is the baked ziti and the tossed salad, Ma. What else do you need me to do?"

"You can put the ziti in the oven to keep warm with the eggplant, chicken cutlets, and mushrooms. Just put out the dishes, cutlery, and the napkins. Then cut up one of the loaves of Italian bread that Tony brought for anyone who wants bread with the hot food. The other three loaves can be used for sandwiches with the white and rye bread. Then you can put out the cold cuts, cheeses, and condiments. Wait until our guests come to put out the food from the oven."

Johnny, as usual, was impressed with his mother-in-law. "Wow, Mom, you haven't missed a beat."

Father Tony always liked Johnny, dating back to the first time he was introduced to the NYPD police officer candidate in 1983. He was always respectful to his mother. He admired how Johnny, as a son-in-law, referred to Teresa Calabrese as Mom. While the kids sought out Seven and Maria assisted her mother, Tony had an opportunity to further converse with Johnny without interruption. He felt the need to have a few questions answered prior to the arrival of the Bathgate/Banks brigade and figured that getting input from the homicide squad Detective was in order.

"Sully, do you ever get involved with cold cases?"

"Not usually, we have a special squad for those, but once in a while when new evidence turns up and it catches the attention of the media, one of my superiors or the DA's office may solicit my squad's input. Why do you ask?"

The priest continued the conversation but was careful to stay within the boundaries of the Seal of Confession. Nothing attributable to the revelations of Andy Miller was discussed.

The doorbell was an indicator of the influx of four houseguests.

Soon, the DVD of *The Blues Brothers* rented by Maria Sullivan for the occasion was inserted into the recently purchased DVD player.

Six adults and four young teenagers watched the 1980 classic comedy starring John Belushi and Dan Aykroyd.

While the portrayal of Jake and Elwood Blues, by Belushi and Aykroyd respectively, thoroughly entertained the four young teens, Father Tony expounded on his knowledge of the duo's inception.

"The Blues Brothers first appeared on *Saturday Night Live* in 1976, and the band also made a few more appearances on the show in the late seventies. John Belushi and Dan Aykroyd also performed live onstage as the Blues Brothers. How do you guys like the music and the dancing of Jake and Elwood?"

After the movie, Johnny Sullivan offered a fact about Father Tony and himself.

"Father Tony and I have performed our impersonation of the Blues Brothers dancing at several weddings."

Tommy Sullivan was impressed. "No kidding, Dad. How about a demonstration?"

"Yeah, Dad," added Tammy. "I'm sure that Scott and Becky would like to see it also."

Maria provided support for her husband and brother. "Those two go crazy when they mimic the Blues Brothers.

They pretty much take over the entire dance floor, and nobody seems to mind because they are extremely good. There is not enough room in here for them to strut around properly, though."

Scott Banks offered a potential solution. His comment was directed at Tammy and Tommy.

"Well, maybe if our grandparents get married, we can see your dad and Father Tony do their thing."

The innocuous comment was overheard by all. Donna Banks was not pleased by her son's remark but realized it was not meant to be offensive. She glanced at her father, and he just smiled and shrugged his shoulders.

Then, with his smile broadening, "What do you think, Teresa?

It wouldn't be right to disappoint the kids."

Tony realized that his mother was a little embarrassed and chose to change the subject.

"I think it is time to have some food and drink. Then, we can put on the pregame show."

As everyone began to fill their plates from the buffet-style setting on the dining room table, Donna Banks decided to have a little fun with the priest who had dominated her thoughts since their near-assignation on the cruise.

"Well, Father Tony, why didn't you and Johnny show off some of your moves on the Royal Caribbean?"

Maria answered on behalf of the two closest males in her life.

"Believe me, Donna. They are both show-offs. If the opportunity presented itself, I'm sure you would have seen a duplication of Jake and Elwood in action. Johnny, go get the framed picture that I bought you for your birthday several years ago and show it to Donna."

"Yes, dear, your wish is my command."

Johnny returned, and Donna perused the photo. "So which one of you is Jake?"

Johnny Sullivan responded to the inquiry, "Father Tony is Jake, and I'm Elwood. I think the first time we performed our act was at my wedding."

"What do you mean *your wedding*, Mr. Hot Shot?" Maria admonished her husband, and then as her brother laughed at the scolding, she further enlightened Donna regarding the skills of her brother.

"Dancing and pitching were what Tony always did best." Scott Banks became curious over the pitching comment. "Father Tony, you were a good pitcher?"

Tommy proudly replied on behalf of his uncle, "He pitched for Manhattan College. He was fantastic, Scott. He would have been in the Major Leagues if he didn't hurt his arm."

Johnny, rebounding from his wife's rebuke, was always ready to support a discussion about the prowess of his brother-in-law as a pitcher.

"You kids certainly have heard of Craig Biggio and Mo Vaughn. What about John Valentin? Well, those three Major leaguers all played for Seton Hall College when Father Tony pitched for Manhattan. In one game, a two-hit shutout, Tony struck out fourteen batters, and none of the three Major leaguers ever reached first base."

"How come Father Tony never went to the Majors?" inquired Scott.

"He hurt his arm just before he graduated from college and needed to be operated on," added Tommy.

"He would have been picked in the first round of the baseball draft had he not sustained that injury" was Johnny's follow-up.

Paul Bathgate was extremely impressed and joined the conversation. "You have quite a fan club, Father Tony."

Donna smiled. "You never mentioned anything about your exploits on the baseball diamond when we were on the cruise." There was one last baseball tidbit from Johnny. "Pete Harnisch was another guy who Father Tony was a contemporary of. He was a star pitcher for Fordham University and was drafted in the first round the year Father Tony graduated. He had real good success in the Major Leagues and pitched for the Mets awhile. Father Tony and Pete Harnisch were always mentioned as the top two pitchers in the New York metropolitan area in their senior year in college."

Another few minutes transpired before Tony was able to interject.

"Thanks for the compliments about my pitching. I would suggest to our guests that they were somewhat aggrandized." "*Aggrandized*? C'mon, Father Tony," chortled a smiling brother-in-law. "Don't start using words like your sister when she tries to impress me with her vocabulary."

The modesty of Father Tony and the obvious devotion of his family further astonished Donna Banks. The fact that the handsome and fit Catholic priest was so comforting on the cruise regarding the loss of her husband had already left an irrevocable impression on the attractive mother of two. The thought of being with another man had not been important to her since her bereavement. Father Anthony Calabrese instilled a revitalization of her desire. *If only he weren't a priest*, she thought to herself.

The girls, Tammy Sullivan and Becky Banks, began sharing stories regarding their respective girls' basketball teams. It was entertaining to all gathered until Becky revealed that she was heckled by an opposing team's father.

"I wish my dad were there," she lamented. "He would have taken care of that loud mouth."

Donna Banks was hearing the story for the first time. Her girlfriend had taken Becky and her own daughter to the game. "What did he say, Becky? Which team was that? Do you play them again? I will be sure to go with you. I'll give him a piece of my mind."

Father Tony offered to attend also. Johnny Sullivan seconded the thought and indicated he would help in any way that Becky needed.

Paul Bathgate was upset on behalf of his granddaughter. "It's my place to be there for Becky, and I will be."

"I want to be there too," added Scott. "She is my sister, and Dad would want me to."

"He is a lot bigger than you, Scott, and much younger than you, Grandpa. I don't want either of you to be hurt."

Father Tony supported Paul Bathgate and Scott and offered a story from his baseball-playing days.

"I remember my dad reacting to a heckler at one of my baseball games in high school. He was in the stands with my sister, and there was a guy trying to get under my skin as I was pitching."

"The guy was big, probably six feet three inches and about 230 pounds and was just being a real idiot, even uttering several highly inappropriate words with young kids and females around. It got worse when Maria complained and told him that she was my sister and he had better tone it down. That revelation only made him more of a jerk."

Maria Sullivan, who had been in the kitchen while her husband and son extolled the pitching proficiency of her brother, recalled the story.

"When that guy told me to 'Be quiet, babe' and 'I don't need to listen to a broad whining about her brother,' my father became incensed."

"Do you want to tell the rest of the story, sis?" "No, Tony, I'm sorry I interrupted. You finish."

"Well, my dad was five feet ten inches tall and weighed 175 pounds. He was strong, though, and was a boxer when he was in the army. He politely asked the guy to calm down and indicated that he was disrespecting his daughter and that it was his son who was pitching. The guy started screaming at him, 'So what are you going to do about it if I don't?'"

A proud son continued, "There were two big hits. First my dad's right fist hit the jaw of the blowhard, and then the second hit was the guy who was five inches taller and over fifty pounds heavier than my dad hitting the floor."

"Way to go Grandpa Calabrese."

"You said it, Tammy." Her brother was equally impressed when hearing the exploits of their mother's dad.

"Is he still alive, Tammy?"

"No, Becky, he died before my brother and I were born."

Donna Banks promised to advise her father if there would be another game against the team with the detractor.

Just then, the phone rang. Teresa Calabrese soon beckoned her son. "Anthony, it's Father Carlos."

Father Tony agreed to meet his mentor the following day for lunch and, upon returning, advised his nephew, "Put the Giants on, Tommy, it's time for us to win our third Super Bowl." A third quarter kickoff return for a touchdown reducing the Raven lead to 17–7 provided the Giants patronage with a momentary glimmer of hope. Unfortunately, the ensuing Giants kickoff resulted in a similar outcome, and Baltimore regained their seventeen-point lead.

One person in the group was thankful for the glorification he received during the Super Bowl, an event that advertisers considered more important than any other and paid for accordingly. In similar fashion to the adulation of Father Tony on the mound, Paul Bathgate was heaped with praise relative to the quality of the Budweiser commercials he assisted in creating. The Budweiser and Budweiser Light advertisements were each viewed enthusiastically.

"They were fantastic, Paul. I just loved them."

A loving son viewed the authenticity of his mother's smile and meandered over to his sister. "Mom probably would have praised the commercials even if she felt they stunk," he whispered.

Father Tony was not pleased about the performance of his football team as he lay in bed thinking that evening. He realized that the Giants had made an excellent account of themselves in the 2000 NFL season up to the playing of Super Bowl XXXV, however, and that in looking at the pigskin encounter that day, they were second best to a better team.

Thoughts of Donna Banks then surfaced. It was evident to him that she was not only a beautiful woman but also a loving mother and daughter. His contemplations were not sexual in nature. That scared the parish priest even more. He was falling in love with her.

"Help me, Lord."

4

Frank's Burger Haven was the lunchtime meeting place for Father Carlos and Father Tony. Two bacon cheeseburger deluxe specials and a pint each of Heineken Light comprised the food and drink for the Catholic priests' early afternoon dialogue.

"I know you bet on the Giants, Tony, I hope you didn't lose too much."

"I was playing with house money, Father Carlos, no worries. You sounded a little discombobulated yesterday on the phone, what's up?"

"I am being transferred to Philadelphia next month. It was approved by the Bishop yesterday morning."

The next half an hour was replete with insight of the findings of Father Carlos regarding the molestation of young boys by a Catholic priest who served with him in his parish. He recounted to Tony that he had first learned of the sexual transgressions during the priest's confession to him over a year before. He noted that he was finally released by the sexual offender relative to the Seal of Confession and was then able to act.

"It took me almost a year to convince Father X to allow me to make the facts public. I don't want to use his real name. He needed professional help, and he finally understood it was for the best. During the last eleven months, we talked twice a week, and I was able to keep the boys he had abused safe from further episodes. I kept a diary that kept track of our conversations, and I have now convinced my pastor and the Bishop to be fully transparent with the parents of the children that were affected. I guess my actions were fruitful, because I have been asked to head a task force for the Archdiocese of Philadelphia."

"No wonder you were so knowledgeable regarding the Seal of Confession. The information you gave me was extremely helpful."

"Listen, Anthony, the vow not to reveal what we learn in the confessional can be extremely difficult to abide by. I pray that you are never faced with a situation that you cannot resolve." Father Tony then confided in Father Carlos regarding Donna Banks. He was fully forthcoming.

"Are your feelings of the flesh, Anthony?"

"She is beautiful to me as a person and in appearance, Father Carlos. I think my initial attraction was based on the fact that she reminded me of Angela. Now I see Donna as her own person, a loving mother, devoted daughter, and sincere woman."

"You tragically lost someone you were in love with, Anthony. I have realized for quite some time that being chaste has not been an easy vow for you to espouse. Now if you are telling me that your sexual desires for this woman are secondary to a true love for her, I suggest you reflect on the reasons that fostered your decision to enter the priesthood and the declarations of faith you made at your ordination. Your love must first and foremost be with the Lord, Jesus Christ."

Father Carlos then offered Father Anthony Calabrese the advice that he was already cognizant of: avoiding her company if possible and prayer. The latter would be followed devoutly. The former, quelling his feelings for Donna and limiting the instances in which their paths would cross, particularly with the budding relationship of his mother and Donna's father, near impossible.

"Remember, I will only be a phone call away if you need me. I suspect that my stay in Philadelphia will be between six to twelve months, then I will be back performing in a similar role for the Diocese of Brooklyn. We must be ardent as Catholic priests to insure the well-being of our youth, particularly from our own. I believe that is my new calling."

"You are truly a remarkable priest and have always been there for me. I am extremely grateful to have you as a confidant and will likely seek your guidance many times in the future."

"Thank you for your confidence in me, Anthony. May God bless us both."

Chapter VII

Cold Case

1

"Hello, son, do you think you can come for dinner tomorrow?"
"Sure, Mom, anything I should know about?"
"No, Anthony, I just need to talk with you and Maria."
"Is seven o'clock good?"
"Make it six thirty if you can."
"Sure thing, Ma, see you then. I'll bring a bottle of Pinot Grigio."

Earlier on that Wednesday, Valentine's Day morning, Teresa Calabrese had received two dozen long-stemmed roses from Paul Bathgate. The note inside apologized for being in Chicago on business, thereby preventing him from taking her to dinner for the occasion, and concluded with "I will make it up to you. All my love, Paul."

2

Teresa Calabrese greeted her son warmly on his arrival. An equally demonstrative reception from Maria and Seven followed.

"I know that Johnny won't be home until seven thirty, and the twins are upstairs doing their homework. I wanted to talk to my daughter and son alone."

After showing Maria and Tony the roses and accompanying note from Paul Bathgate, she was guarded with her words. "What do you two think?"

The elder sibling spoke first. "Beautiful, Ma," said Maria, and then with a broad smile, she continued, "I got nothing from Johnny so far." Then, sipping from the glass of Pinot Grigio just poured by her brother, she added, "Paul is a good guy, and he cares for you. What do you want to talk about?"

"I think I am falling in love with him, and it scares me. We've only known each other for six weeks. It just seems crazy to me. I feel like I would like to have your approval. I sense that he may be thinking of giving me a ring in the near future."

Tony sought to lighten the moment. "A ring? What do you mean, a phone call, so what's the big deal?"

Maria tried in vain not to laugh but failed. "You are a real jerk, Tony. Mom is serious."

"Oh, I get it, Ma, an engagement ring. I think you should tell him that it better be at least two carats."

"Idiot!" said Maria, looking askew toward her brother and then directing her response to the woman who gave birth to her. "You two seem to complement each other, Ma. Anyway, you don't need our permission on this. Dad has been gone over thirteen years. He would want you to be happy."

"Maria is right, Mother dear. If he pops the question, do you know anyone who can perform the wedding ceremony?"

"You are just a real idiot."

"It's OK, Maria, your brother could always make me laugh. I am just glad that both of you are comfortable with the potential of me getting married again someday."

A week and a half later, two orchestra seats at *Phantom of the Opera* preceded a late dinner at Sardi's.

The following morning on the way to Sunday Mass with Maria, Johnny, and the kids, Teresa pulled her daughter aside.

"I do love him, Maria."

Later that day, Maria informed Johnny of her mother's feelings for Paul Bathgate. The law enforcement professional responded to his wife.

"I think I should do a background check on him just in case.

I wouldn't want your mom to ever be hurt."

"OK, but please discuss your intentions with my brother first."

3

The attempt of Father Tony to somewhat deviously obtain additional information from Johnny regarding cold-case investigations culminated without recourse of new ideas. He remained hopeful of learning more from Andy Miller; his curiosity was piqued.

Fortunately, the priest had several matters that occupied his time in addition to his responsibilities at St. John the Baptist parish. He was happy yet concerned about his mother and awaited his brother-in-law's due diligence on the character and background of Paul Bathgate. The travel baseball team arrangements were underway, and Donna Banks was continually in his thoughts.

The vetting of his prospective stepfather had a conclusion that was pleasing to Tony. Johnny privately made the revelation. "Listen, Father Tony, I have already told Maria what I am about to say. The guy is aces from everything I've learned. Your mom has nothing to worry about regarding his character. He's got some bucks too. There is one thing that was a little surprising to me since he never brought it up, but then maybe he has already spoken to Teresa about it. He has a thirty-seven- year-old son who lives in San Francisco. He is on the police force there."

"Donna did tell me she had an older brother, but we never really got into it," added Tony.

4

Saturday, March 17, St. Patrick's Day

Father Tony visited the grave of Angela Santino. It was hard to believe that it had been fourteen years since the fateful day of her tragic demise.

"Fourteen years already, Hoops."

Back at the Calabrese household, his mother hurried to answer the telephone as Seven happily paraded at her feet.

"Hello, Teresa, Paul. The reservation at Patrick's Pub is for seven p.m. I'll pick you up at six thirty."

The dinner was quite different than the Italian cuisine the two usually enjoyed together. The sharing of shepherd's pie as an appetizer followed by a traditional St. Paddy's Day fare of corned beef and cabbage was a pleasant variation.

A visit to the ladies' room by Teresa Calabrese after her meal afforded Paul Bathgate with the opportunity to have a surprise awaiting her return.

The two-carat custom-cut pear-shaped Neil Lane-designed stone was graciously accepted by Teresa with an "I will, Paul, I will" after his "Teresa Calabrese, will you marry me?" request.

The two decided not to say anything until Sunday, when Paul, Donna, Scott, and Becky would join the Calabrese clan for dinner.

The dining room table was replete with the gastronomy of the Calabrese culture. Two kinds of homemade ravioli, one with just ricotta cheese and the second also including broccoli rabe, were complimented by the meatballs made from the secret recipe of Teresa's mother and the sweet and hot sausage from Benito's butcher shop. A pork roast, a large green salad, and Tony's favorite, stuffed artichokes, added to the Sunday family eat-a-thon, a description first coined by Tommy Sullivan.

"So how was dinner at Patrick's Pub last night?" Johnny Sullivan, who often frequented the establishment with his police brethren, made the inquiry.

"It was lovely Johnny. Paul and I enjoyed it immensely. Excuse me for a minute, though, I want to get a few other types of salad dressing for the kids. They may not want the olive oil and red wine vinegar."

Teresa had hidden the engagement ring in a little-used kitchen cabinet. She placed it on her finger and returned with blue cheese and french dressings.

"Hey, Grandma, what's that on your finger?" inquired Tammy. "Oh, I won that cute ring at a raffle and gave it to your grandmother last night," interjected Paul Bathgate with a smile.

Maria was curious. "Let me see that, Mom. Oh my God, oh my God."

She hugged her mother so hard that the loving gesture nearly caused a loss of breath.

"Maria, you're killing me."

"Dad, this is wonderful. I am so happy for both of you," bellowed Donna Banks.

Father Tony kissed and hugged his mother and then shook the hand of his stepfather-to-be.

As the congratulations continued from Johnny, Tammy, Tommy, Scott, and Becky, Father Anthony Calabrese thought to himself, *Unbelievable, Donna will be my stepsister!*

5

Andy Miller visited the volunteer NYPD chaplain several days later. His disclosures regarding additional facts were restrained. "Listen, Father Tony, I spoke with my mother. There is more to tell you, but not here. I want my words to be protected. I will talk to you again this Saturday in confession."

Saturday could not come soon enough for the priest, but he had no recourse other than to wait for the officer who had confided in him. Patience is a virtue, one not found in the makeup of Father Tony. His thoughts were sundry. Should he discuss any information he may learn with his brother-in-law? Could he do so without violating his vow? Was it possible that Andy Miller had information about the events that resulted in Angela's death?

That Saturday, the confessional never saw the presence of Andrew Miller. Father Anthony Calabrese was at a loss as to what alternatives he had to foster the revelation of facts from the NYPD patrolman.

6

"There is a phone call for you, Father Tony."

The Saturday evening interruption was not typical in the rectory, but the priest answered the call with the expectation of hearing the voice of his mother.

"Hi, Father Tony, it's Donna Banks."

The priest felt an excitement similar to having a girlfriend return his phone call when he was a teenager. The tone of his response was subdued, however, as he endeavored to disguise his exuberant emotions.

"How are you, Donna? How can I help you this evening?"

"I wanted to get your thoughts on arranging to have an engagement party for your mom and my dad and also get your sister's phone number to solicit her opinion."

The conversation continued briefly; Tony was pleasant but circumspect. He indicated that he would like to share in the cost of any celebration and gave Donna the telephone number of Maria.

"I am sure that the two of you can come up with arrangements for the festivities. Let me know if you need my input with anything."

Just before the phone call, Father Tony's focus was on what he might learn from Andy Miller; now the image of Donna Banks subjugated his thought process.

7

The diminutive engagement party gathering of immediate family and a few special friends proved to be insightful for the son of the bride-to-be.

"Hi, you must be Father Tony, I'm Jeremy Bathgate. My dad and sister are always talking about you with admiration. I feel that I know you."

"You are lucky to have a father and sister like those two. I am happy to meet you, Jeremy."

Shortly thereafter, the two were sharing sport stories, specifically, several of the notable encounters between the San Francisco 49ers and New York Giants. Then, the inclination of Jeremy Bathgate was to reveal personal information.

"I moved to the West Coast in 1986, right after I graduated from Columbia. A classmate of mine grew up in San Francisco and coerced me into moving. My parents and sister were not very pleased, but I was sick of the New York City winters.

"By the way, Father, I am bisexual and was estranged from the family from just after college until six or seven years ago. My dad always had difficulty with my sexual orientation. Thank God for Mom and Donna. They convinced him to be more open minded."

"Have you ever been in a serious relationship?"

"I was married to a woman for a year. She soon realized that I also had a fondness for men and could never get past it. Then, I moved in with that classmate I referred to earlier and that lasted about six months."

"What happened?

"He wasn't pleased when he found me in bed with his sister." "Wow, Jeremy, and I thought I had problems."

"My dad is enamored with the fact that I am seeing a woman again and that I have indicated that it may be getting serious. I decided it best that she stay in San Francisco, but you never know, maybe you will be meeting her at the wedding."

"Listen, Jeremy, if you ever need someone to talk to, I am your man, or perhaps I should say, I am your priest."

"Hey, sis, you're right about this guy, he has a sense of humor and is a good listener."

Donna Banks knew the feeling well. "Go mingle, Jeremy, I want to speak with Father Tony."

The priest smiled at Donna and indicated that his conversation with her brother was both enlightening and enjoyable.

"Let him go talk to Johnny," requested Donna. "They have a lot in common. I am sure he mentioned that he is working for the San Francisco PD. He's a forensic specialist."

"That's interesting, he didn't mention that to me."

The sit-down Sunday afternoon setting of three tables of ten at Angelo's restaurant near the Queens/Long Island border afforded an opportunity for the priest to sit between Donna and Jeremy. He commenced the revelry with a meal blessing and a heartfelt acknowledgement that his mother had found, as he put it, "a second soul mate."

Father Tony now had an agenda that was not initially envisioned. Whenever the enticing female to his left was preoccupied by a question from Maria or Johnny, the inquiry of police work involving unsolved cases were issues he discussed with Jeremy. The SFPD forensic specialist expounded on his knowledge of the subject, additionally conveying his involvement with two cold-case investigations requiring his expertise.

Tony was pleased that he might now have an alternative to involving his brother-in-law; it was Jeremy. He felt this would reduce the chances of any violation to his vow regarding the Seal of Confession. The final inquiry on the topic was done in little more than a whisper. He was careful that his request was not overheard.

"Jeremy, do you mind if I give you a call sometime regarding cold-case investigations? I have a parishioner who is taking a criminal justice class and is doing a term paper."

"Sure, Father Tony. I'll give you my home number."

He then thought to himself. *A little white lie, that's all. Just a little white lie.*

Chapter VIII

It's Miller Time

1

The Easter Sunday dinner at the Calabrese household was laden with conversation regarding the plans of Teresa and Paul relative to tying the knot.

The wedding had been planned without haste. Teresa Calabrese and Paul Bathgate would be married in Curacao during Memorial Day weekend, a destination wedding that included predominantly family members. Paul added two former business partners and their wives to the attendee list.

The generous groom had just shy of two million Marriott points and saw the hotel, with an exquisite variety of wedding options, as the perfect opportunity to provide rooms for all the invitees. A wedding planner was retained by the groom to minimize the efforts of Donna and Maria. Each was frantic that everything for their respective parents would be flawless.

Father Tony would perform the wedding service on the beach and would be assisted by Father Carlos. The son of the bride wanted to escort his mother to the altar, and the assistance of Father Carlos to commence the religious episode for the Catholic widow and widower was deemed to be expedient. The two priests would also share a room, a development encouraged by Tony.

That should alleviate any potential temptation with Donna, he thought.

The revelation that Donna would be sharing a room with her first cousin gave Father Tony additional comfort.

Paul Bathgate's munificence extended beyond providing lodging for the Easter dinner gathering; airplane tickets were also purchased for all. The flight to Curacao would additionally be made available for his son, Jeremy, his girlfriend, and Father Carlos.

"My sister is so excited for me," exclaimed Teresa. We haven't seen each other in almost two years. She can't wait to meet Paul and see the family again. Can you believe she has been down in Naples for three years already?"

"Aunt Stella will love Paul, Ma, and speaking of Naples, a Florida trip is definitely on the to-do list."

"Is Stella as pretty as your mom?" inquired the future husband of Teresa Calabrese.

"She's pretty, but not as pretty as Mom," interjected Maria.

"Aunt Stella can still fill out a pair of jeans for a sixty-three-year-old woman."

"Anthony, I am surprised at you, and on Easter Sunday no less."

"Sorry, Ma, just having a little fun."

Donna tried not to chuckle as everyone else at the dinner table shared amusement.

The priest peered at the enchanting woman who aroused in him feelings similar to those of a distant past and transiently thought of how her taut buttocks would fill out a pair of jeans. He closed his eyes, and the memory of her derriere in the red two-piece bathing suit that had mesmerized him on the cruise gave him his answer.

2

Andy Miller sat at the kitchen table with his mother, Tina.

"Are you sure that it was Alex who had taken Dad's gun?"

"I can't be positive, Andrew, but I have always suspected it. Your father left us in 1986, and the gun was in the attic. He had called me and said that he had forgotten it and to make sure you kids didn't get your hands on it. He told me that the gun was in a locked box and that the key was in our top drawer dresser. I checked for the box about a year later, and it was gone. Alex is the only one who could have taken it."

"Did you ask him about it?"

"He said that he didn't know what I was talking about and that he never even knew that Dad had a gun. I knew that was a lie. Your father told me that he had shown the gun to Alex when he was younger."

"Not that it is going to be of any use, but do you still have the key?"

"Yes, and I have the gun permit."

"You have the permit for Dad's gun? That's good, Ma. I'll take it."

"All right, Andrew, I'll get it now."

3

The Sunday promise of a weekday lunch with Donna Banks at the Italian restaurant, Arturo's, just east of the Cross Island Parkway on NY 25 in the neighborhood of Floral Park offered a temporary reprieve from the unfolding murder mystery. Unfortunately, the get-together with his stepsister-to-be, under the presumption of discussing the impending marriage of their respective parents, renewed his confrontation with the vow of celibacy.

The lunch, which saw the captivating Ms. Banks enjoy shrimp parmigiana and the former Manhattan College pitching stalwart taking pleasure in his veal *sorrentino*, was a comfortable experience for both until the pronouncement of Donna about her accommodations for the wedding.

"I was hoping to room with my cousin, Christine, when we go to Curacao, but she has to cancel because she has nobody to watch her five-year-old daughter. I will be by myself. The kids will continue to stay as planned, Becky with Tammy and Scott with Tommy."

Father Tony remained calm, at least on the outside. His expression was that of the poker face he had learned to master during his college days, when his card-playing prowess provided him with more earnings than his part-time job at his uncle's hardware store. He knew his reply would need to be indicative of this demeanor.

"Well, if she is a snorer," said the smiling cleric, "you won't have to worry about that now."

On his drive back to the St. John the Baptist rectory, Father Tony thought of the additional possible temptation, that is, the beautiful woman whom he was very attracted to rooming alone.

"That's all I need."

He found a message on his return. It was from the coordinator of the NYPD volunteer chaplain group requesting his presence the following morning at 10:00 a.m. He called to confirm his attendance.

4

The word at the police department had spread. Father Anthony Calabrese was the priest to talk to if you had an issue that required celestial intervention. Many officers, other than Catholics, sought his intercession. Protestants, Jews, Muslims, agnostics, and even an atheist were comforted by Father Tony. Andy Miller was one of several police officers that Chaplain Anthony Calabrese spoke with during his morning volunteer encounter. Unfortunately, his visit was only to indicate that he would speak with the priest that Saturday afternoon in confession. The weekend could not come soon enough for the priest.

"Bless me, Father . . ."; it was Andy. "I spoke with my mother, and she agreed that I should let you know that our concern for Alex stems from his reckless behavior in high school and after he graduated. He always had money, lots of money, much more than he ever could have earned working for the liquor distributor. He was drinking all of the time and carousing around in his red Mustang. He always loved his cars, and they were always Mustangs, and they were always red."

The priest listened attentively. Andy further conveyed recollections of the sinister behavior of his brother, several leading to arrests for excessive speeding and driving while intoxicated.

"He went crazy when his driver's license was suspended. My mom felt that a felony conviction was in the near future. She would always hear Alex talking to his friends about how it was like 'taking candy from a baby.' She suspected he was into robberies, but he always denied it when she questioned him. She reached out to a good family friend who helped get Alex into the army just before he turned twenty. I was fourteen at the time, by the way. He served for three years and then worked in my uncle's deli in Yonkers. Then he took the police exam and did well, and the extra military credits put him high enough on the list to be selected for the academy in 1993. He's been a cop ever since."

"So now what, Andy? Why are you and your mom so concerned, and why are you telling me all this?"

"I reviewed the file on the liquor store robbery case in Bay Ridge, Brooklyn. The one on March 17, 1987."

Father Anthony Calabrese was speechless. He twirled his sideburns with his fingers, a longtime habit when he was in deep thought. He awaited the continuation of Andy's disclosure. "The robbery involved the theft of ten cases of expensive liquors, mostly high-end champagnes, imported wines, and top-shelf scotch and whiskey. All the cases were still on pallets in the back of the store, having just been delivered earlier in the day. The police report indicated that it was apparent that the robbers were cognizant of the shipment and that there were an additional ten cases, which were more than likely to be included in the theft if not for an interruption from within the store proper. The victims of the shootings were Jerry Talbot, nineteen, son of the store owner, Mike Talbot, who was working the cash register that evening and found in the rear store room.

When notified, the grieving owner indicated to police that he had just left the premises a half an hour before."

Andy Miller continued his dialogue, offering details relative to another victim of the armed robbery.

"The second victim was a customer, Angela Santino, twenty-one, who was apparently struck by one of the bullets intended for the nineteen-year-old. A bullet hole was found in the backroom sheetrock wall, and the speculation was that it had passed through and innocently struck the young woman. Each victim was pronounced dead at the scene. There were no witnesses to the shooting, but the case file reveals an elaborate discussion with the boyfriend of Angela Santino, who had dropped her off to purchase a few bottles for a St. Patrick's Day dinner. That would be you, Father, Anthony Calabrese."

Andy concluded his "confession" with a pertinent observation.

"My brother worked for a liquor distributor from 1986 to 1988. He delivered to Bay Ridge Liquors."

Father Tony was at a loss for words, partly because of a lack of understanding with regard to investigative procedures.

"What does that prove, Andy?"

"Nothing, Father, but I have information about the weapon used that evening based on the forensic analysis of the bullets retrieved from the victims."

"So..."

Andy Miller then revealed the conversation with his mother relative to his dad's gun and that he had a copy of the gun permit.

"The bullets were determined to have come from the type of revolver my dad had."

"Oh my God, Andy. You have to give me the OK to discuss this. I want to have my brother-in-law get involved. You may know him, Detective Johnny Sullivan."

"No, Father, I won't grant you permission, not yet anyway. I am trying to get authorization to review if there were other liquor store robberies in the area from 1986 through 1988. I want to focus in Brooklyn and Queens, which was Alex's territory. I also want to take a look at the case file for the liquor store robbery in Sheepshead Bay, where my brother shot and killed the two teenage perps at the end of last year."

"So you are restricting me from assisting you. I find that strange. Do you really want to know if your brother has had an involvement, or are you just going through the motions? What is your end game here?"

"I want to clear my conscience, but this is not an easy thing for me. It's my brother we are talking about. My mother is struggling with this also."

"Do the right thing, my son."

Upon the completion of the afternoon confessions, Father Anthony Calabrese left the confessional with the knowledge that he may know the identity of Angela's murderer. He now also knew that her death was evidently accidental. He was confused that this information had never been brought to light; his resultant feelings regarding the loss of his fiancée-to-be, however, were unchanged. "It should have been me."

Father Tony deliberated on follow-up actions. How could he discuss this information with Johnny without violating the Seal of Confession? There had to be a way. He decided to re- review the Catholic Church teachings he had received from Father Carlos.

That evening, Father Tony spent several hours praying in the rectory chapel.

5

Father Tony served the early Mass the following day. He was distraught regarding the more specific knowledge of Angela's death, and he wanted to be able to speak with Johnny about it.

The gathering of St. John the Baptist parishioners listened to a homily not typical of any priest.

"I am a sinner, just like you. Don't ever think that you are alone in the battle against the devil. Priests share in the daily combat to overcome temptation and lead a Christlike life. As I stand before you, I ask for your prayers and pledge to be with you as you face your own hardships."

The dialogue was heartfelt and apparently hit home with many of those in attendance. As the priest completed the service and walked to the back of the church, a throng of almost one hundred waited to greet him and convey their appreciation for his honest, down-to-earth approach. A typical pronouncement was "Father Tony, thank you. I will keep you in my prayers."

Later that morning, Tony knew where he had to go. It had been over two weeks since he had visited the graves of Angela and his father. His first stop at Calvary Cemetery was his dad.

"I wish I still had you around, Pop. It seems as if I am in a constant battle with my feelings. Making the right decision on several matters is a burden on my brain. Listen, Dad, Mom and sis really miss you also. I also wanted to say that Mom knows that Paul will never replace you, he will just add to the love, respect, and care you had always provided. Oh yeah, When you get a chance, pray for me."

Several sections over, Anthony Calabrese parked his car again. In a minute, he stood in front of the grave of Angela Santino.

"Hey, Hoops, I still love you and always will. I found out recently that your getting shot was an accident. This revelation only makes me feel worse. It should have been me. I am so, so sorry."

Tony looked up and smiled. He wondered for a moment why almost everyone associated looking skyward as a means to view a loved one who has passed away. Heaven is up and hell is down. The Grey Nuns of the Sacred Heart in grammar school must have taught him that, he thought.

"Well, I know you are up there, Angela, and I need your help. Remember when I dropped you off at the liquor store, did you notice anything unusual? I recall you pointedly reminding me of getting you the ring. I still recall the request. 'At least one carat, pear shaped or round stone, size 7.'"

Tony had his eyes closed now. His focus was exclusively on recollections of the St. Patrick's Day evening in 1987.

"Oh, that's right, you were busting me about my Camaro before that, saying I would give a ring to the car before I gave one to you. You also said something else before you entered the liquor store. It was about another car, I think."

Tony paused and removed old flowers, replacing them with a fresh bouquet. He added water to the vaselike metal-spiked container from the bucket he had filled.

"Angela, it was a red Mustang, right? What were you pointing out to me? Something had your interest. C'mon, Hoops, help me remember."

Perhaps it was Angela looking for closure; maybe it was divine intervention. In any event, the results were evident.

"The bumper sticker and the coasters along the rear dashboard, they were for Miller beer. They read Miller Time or It's Miller Time. Oh my God, a red mustang with an association to Miller Time. Too much of a coincidence not to be . . . just had to be . . . you can't tell me I'm wrong . . . *Alex Miller*! Thanks, Angela Bella."

6

It was a week before Mother's Day. The previous morning, Father Tony had been the beneficiary of a tip from an astute horse-racing buff on the Kentucky Derby, which proved to be profitable. He was in as good a mood as could be expected. On his way to the family residence just after noon, Father Tony wondered if he might have an opening in overcoming his Seal of Confession restriction. The fact that he learned of the red Mustang ownership of Alex Miller through his brother's confessional disclosure in conjunction with his divine recall of events preceding the shooting of Angela was instrumental in Father Tony's resolve to continue his investigative process.

How can I talk about this with Sully without violating the seal? he thought to himself,

The priest was greeted by a four-legged, tail-waving, playful puppy. Seven was always excited to see Tony. The pup was rewarded with an old tennis ball from his baseball team duffel bag.

"Here, Seven, play with this. When Tommy comes down, he'll play catch with you outside."

"And what do you have for your mother?"

"Well, besides the usual bottle of wine—I brought a bottle of Pinot Noir this time—how about I give you a big hug?"

"That works for me."

A few minutes later, Father Tony was greeting his sister, brother-in-law, and the twins.

"Hey, Tommy, why don't you call Scott? He is officially on our baseball travel team. And here is an old tennis ball for you to play with Seven."

The news was greeted gleefully by his nephew, and Tony was equally enveloped by hugs and kisses form his niece and sister. Johnny patted Tony on the back and handed him a Heineken.

"I'll be a good brother-in-law, for a while anyway, let's watch the Yankees game together. The Mets aren't on until later."

"Hey, sis, how about bringing in something to pick on?"

Tony couldn't wait to petition the NYPD Detective.

"Sully, I need to confide in you. I am going to ask you for a favor but would prefer that you limit the questions as to why I am asking. Is that OK?"

"Sure, Tony. What do you want to ask me?"

"It's about the night Angela was killed."

Father Tony proceeded to explain that he had information regarding the events of the evening that may assist in the identification of the cold-case killer. He requested that Johnny examine the case file and then talk to him. He purposely limited the facts he presented to those learned outside the confessional. The priest felt his actions were in accordance with his vow.

"I'll do it tomorrow and stop over at the rectory after work." "How about I meet you at Benito's Pizzeria at seven p.m., instead?"

"Fine."

7

Father Tony sat in a booth at 6:50 p.m. after ordering a Sicilian pie (half sausage and half pepperoni) and two bottles of Miller Lite. The beer just seemed appropriate for the occasion; he commenced his consumption prior to Johnny's arrival.

"Have a beer, Johnny, the Sicilian pie should be out soon. Whatever we don't eat, you can just take home."

Johnny nodded affirmatively and began to reveal his findings. "I reviewed the case file. It was quite disturbing. Are you sure you want me to tell you what I learned? It will bring back memories that your sister has always told me to avoid talking with you about."

"Thank you for your concern, but yes, I want to hear what you found out."

Everything conveyed about the March 17, 1987, liquor store robbery and killings were facts that Father Tony was previously privy to. The difference, in his mind anyway, was that now he was made cognizant of them outside of the confessional.

"Listen, Sully, yesterday I remembered something about that evening that I never mentioned to the police. I guess that I didn't think that it was important at the time. I do now."

The pizza arrived at the table.

"Good choice, Father, half sausage and half pepperoni. What can I give you?"

The priest took a bite of his selected sausage slice, while the Detective did likewise to the pepperoni. Johnny took a swallow of his Miller Lite and questioned the choice of the cleric.

"I don't think I've seen you drinking a Miller Lite before. Why the selection of hops?"

"The beer I chose coincides with what I am about to tell you." Several minutes of discussion with regard to what had occurred prior to Angela entering the liquor store had Johnny interested but unclear of Tony's intentions.

"What are you trying to tell me, Father Tony?"

"I think that car belonged to Alex Miller. I believe he had an involvement that night."

"Purely circumstantial, Father. What has you thinking this way?"

"Listening to Andy Miller in my role as chaplain."

Twenty-five minutes later, the priest had an agreement that his brother-in-law would seek to speak personally with the Detectives who had been assigned to the investigation in 1987 and also take a closer look at the Sheepshead Bay incident in which Alex Miller had shot and killed two teenagers.

"I'll find out where the two Detectives who investigated the 1987 case are working. Hopefully, neither of them has retired, or with any luck, at least one of them is still around. I'll snoop around regarding the shooting in Sheepshead Bay."

"Thanks, Sully."

Chapter IX

Curacao

1

Father Tony arrived for the Mother's Day dinner at 12:30 p.m. There were several things he needed to do. The review of his mom's gift from him and his sister's family was the first agenda item. He knew of his responsibility to absorb half of the cost of the two dozen red roses and the Tiffany and Company heart pendant, which Maria said she had purchased through a friend. A discussion with Johnny Sullivan was also incumbent.

"Cough up the $200, dear brother."

"The roses are beautiful. Let me see the pendant."

"The scrolls of the design are based on nineteenth-century iron gates."

"OK, sis, I like it, enough with the sales pitch."

The grinning facial expression of Father Tony caused a smiling rebuttal from Maria.

"Two hundred dollars, Tony, and be grateful that you have a sister who can pick out nice things for their mother and save you money doing it."

Tony handed Maria two bills with the image of Benjamin Franklin adorning the front. His $100 wager on the Kentucky Derby winner, Monarchos, the week before had paid over ten to one, so the cash was readily available.

"Is the money compliments of Monarchos, Tony?"

"You got that right, Sully."

Maria had a deliberation that she envisioned would evoke a comment from her brother.

"I should have charged you more if I knew you had cashed in on the Derby."

"OK, sis, here is another dollar. Will that do it, my darling sister, or should I make it two?"

"Wow, a dollar. Do you want a receipt, Mr. Trump? I have to go downstairs now and help Mom. She wanted to prepare everything even though it is her day."

"OK, big sister, I need to talk with your husband before I come down. Don't tell Mom that I am here yet."

As Maria was making her way downstairs, Johnny was ready to reveal his new findings. "OK, Father Tony, let's talk."

Before wishing his mother the adulation due her for giving him birth, the priest listened attentively to what the NYPD Detective had to say. He was ecstatic to learn that Sully had not only spoken with both Detectives assigned to the murders on the St. Patrick's Day of 1987 but that he took it upon himself to investigate the car ownership records of Alex Miller.

Most of the facts from the inquiry were previously known to Father Tony. He found one supporting piece of evidence particularly insightful: the determination that the robbery and shooting was more than likely perpetrated by young and inexperienced offenders. This seemed contradictory to the fact that the heinous incident remained unsolved.

The revelations of vehicle ownership of Alex Miller reflected that four vehicles were registered to him during the years 1986 to present. All four cars were Ford Mustangs. All four cars were red. The first vehicle was model year 1984 and was purchased used at a Ford dealership in Brooklyn. It remained in service through 1993 before being replaced with a new model that year. The research showed another new vehicle in 1997 and a fourth red Mustang in 2000.

"Alex certainly has a love for Mustangs and the color red. From what I hear, he treats the cars with kid gloves."

"So he would have been driving the '84 Mustang on St. Patrick's Day in 1987." "Yes, Tony."

"What were you able to learn about the robbery and shootings in Sheepshead Bay?"

"I am still checking that out. Why is that incident so important to you, Father Tony?"

"You are going to think I am crazy, Sully."

"How so?"

"I think that Alex may have been involved in the robbery. I need some time to collect my thoughts. Can you meet tomorrow night at the pizza place?"

Upon Johnny agreeing to Tony's request, the two made their way down to the first floor.

"Hey, Ma, Happy Mother's Day."

"Anthony, where have you been? Come here and give your mother a big hug."

"Sure thing, Mrs. Calabrese. Have you reflected on the fact that you will soon be Mrs. Bathgate? I like Paul, but I much prefer the name Calabrese to Bathgate."

The appearance of the Bathgate/Banks troop offered news that Father Tony found comforting. Donna Banks's cousin had found a babysitter and would be available to attend the wedding. Donna would once again have a roommate.

One less thing to worry about, thought Tony.

2

Several days later, a pizza place discussion provided the wannabe cop with findings he found supportive of his thinking. Johnny Sullivan offered a myriad of facts that were not known to the public regarding the Sheepshead Bay liquor store shootings.

- The robbery was evidently well planned and made through the back of the store.
- The owner had left the liquor store about an hour before the robbery.
- His employee, an eighteen-year-old, stated that he heard noise coming from the back and called 911.
- Alex and his partner responded in less than five minutes, and Alex went around the back of the store as the second officer entered the front.
- Alex, an excellent marksman, fired two rounds, each bullet entering the chest of the respective perpetrators.
- Alex reported that both of the robbers had guns and discharged his weapon only after warning both to drop theirs. Only one weapon was found, however. This was the principal cause for further investigation. (Father Tony had previously been made aware of this fact.)
- The weapon of the perpetrator, which was retrieved, a Smith & Wesson model, had fired one round, and the bullet matching the gun was found in the back wall of the store. A second bullet was found but did not match that model weapon. Forensics determined that it was from a .38 revolver.
- The perps were seniors at Brooklyn Tech High School, and both were known as very smart and, other than pranks in the classroom, well behaved.

- Alex's partner did not witness the shootings, nor did the store employee.
- A Ford Explorer was found in the rear of the store and had been loaded with over a dozen cases of premium liquors.
- The tailgate was found down, so it was believed that the robbery was still in progress.
- The mother of one of the shooting victims testified that the two were both good kids and often seen with an older friend who had a red car. The model of the car was not known.

3

"Hello there, Father Tony. It's Father Carlos, how are you? I just wanted to give you the update on my plans for your mother's wedding."

The pleasantries between the two holy administrators of the Catholic faith provided further evidence of their special bond. Father Tony thought about bringing up the revelations regarding Angela's death, whose funeral Father Carlos had presided over some fourteen years prior, but decided against it. Father Carlos would arrive in Curacao on the Friday of the wedding weekend and would be required to leave on Sunday morning. He was truly thankful to have been called upon to serve with Father Tony at the late Saturday afternoon wedding Mass service.

"I am so looking forward to seeing you again, Father Carlos."

Tony paused to reflect on what the plans of his mentor in faith meant. The recognition that his own return flight was not until Monday and that the final night of his stay would be without a roommate would open the gates to temptation on his concluding evening on the Caribbean Island.

4

Tammy Sullivan and Becky Banks, the two young teenagers whose respective grandmother and grandfather would soon tie the knot, had become extremely chummy, their thoughts fully transparent.

"My Uncle Tony, I mean, Father Tony, is so happy for my grandma. He thinks your grandfather is great, and he thinks you, your brother, and your mom are the best."

"Well, I love Father Tony. How great it must be to have an uncle who is a really cool priest. My brother says he is the best baseball coach he has ever had, and my mom is always talking about him. I think that if he weren't a priest, she'd be hoping that they were a couple."

5

The first game of the St. John the Baptist travel baseball team was just a week away. The Vikings, coming off a 19–6 season (with a disheartening loss in the League Championship game), had only two boys who were required to leave because of age. The replacements were a twelve-year-old seventh grader who could play multiple infield positions, was a good contact hitter, and had amazing speed and an outfielder/relief pitcher with a big bat. The latter was Scott Banks, Donna's fourteen-year- old son.

The baseball scene was just what the doctor ordered for Father Tony. It was a welcome release from his constant battle to remain true to his vows.

The former standout pitcher at Manhattan College was in his element. He understood the nuances of the game, earned the respect of his players by maintaining a disciplined but fair atmosphere, and always preached the philosophy that "Baseball is just a game, have fun out there."

The last Saturday morning practice was attended by his assistant coach, Johnny Sullivan, and Donna Banks, who had agreed to be the team scorekeeper and maintain adherence to league regulations. Tony was happy to have her since he felt that she would thwart the other mothers from making advances on him. *Better to have just one female distraction,* he thought.

Johnny and Donna got along well. Each was a rooter of the wrong New York baseball team (according to the world of Anthony Calabrese anyway), the Mets.

"Can't you guys face the fact that the Yankees are better? We just kicked your butt in the World Series. The Mets will always be number 2 in the Big Apple."

Father Tony had only one problem with his travel team: the father of the recent twelve-year-old addition to the squad.

He was as Johnny succinctly stated on several occasions, "a pain in the ass."

The priest/manager endeavored to patiently listen to the rants of the parent.

"My son, Danny, is the best second baseman, he should play there."

"He is a great leadoff hitter, have him hitting first in the lineup."

"You have to give Danny jersey number 2, Derek Jeter is his favorite player."

Father Tony knew it was time to take Danny Bailey's father aside. He wasn't about to listen to this crap all year. The other parents were pleased that their manager was taking action; they respected his judgment on how to handle the team and were not inclined to allow a newcomer to upset the applecart. "Sully, do me a favor and take over. I've got to set Mr. Bailey straight."

"I have my gun. Do you want me to fire a warning shot over his head? He'll soil himself and that will be it."

The priest laughed and made his way toward the disruptive culprit. "Mr. Bailey, can we have a word together?"

In a matter of minutes, the issue was resolved. Father Tony was firm but respectful as he outlined the decisions affecting the newcomer to the Vikings.

- Danny Bailey would play second base, the position Tony anticipated him to play anyway.
- He would bat last.
- Number 2 was already taken; he would be given number 22.
- There would be no further comments about the running of the team or his presence at the games would not be welcome.

Case closed!

6

The family dinner prior to the weekend of the wedding included the Bathgate/Banks foursome. Johnny found the ball busting of his brother-in-law by Donna Banks very amusing.

"Listen, Father Tony, Scott has to play center field and bat fourth, and he wants to wear jersey number 24 because his dad taught him all about Willie Mays. He also wants to be the team captain, so can you put a *C* on his uniform? Oh, one last thing, as the team scorekeeper, can you get me a T-shirt with Vikings Assistant Coach written on it, and I'd like a different-colored hat. Can you get me pink?"

Maria Sullivan was hysterical and offered the support she felt compelled to add as Donna's future stepsister. The two women had grown extremely close as they painstakingly assisted with the arrangements for the wedding of their respective parents. "Way to go, Donna, Scott will be part of the family, and the requests for him sound reasonable, and as far as what you asked for yourself, they are also very rational in my mind."

Father Tony's grin was evident as he inquired, "Would you like a pink Vikings hat also, sis?"

Tammy Sullivan jumped up and put her arms around her uncle. "Can you get the pink hats for Becky and me too?"

"OK, Ms. Banks, see what you've started. Pour me some wine, Sully. I can see that the ladies are going to be relentless today."

Father Tony was impressed with the humor of Donna Banks. He now saw a beautiful woman with a wit previously unbeknownst to him.

"I think Donna has your number," observed his mother.

The camaraderie between the families was apparent. There were ten exuberant participants in the ensuing discussion regarding the destination wedding of Teresa Calabrese and Paul Bathgate.

Donna was inquisitive that afternoon and confided in her newest female companion, Maria, as the two were alone in the kitchen after the completion of the meal.

"Maria, I was curious about what Father Tony was like before he became a priest."

"My brother was a real womanizer until he met Angela. She knew how to put him in his place, and he needed that. Actually, I think he grew to like it."

"Did you think she was right for him?"

"Absolutely, they were perfect together. You remind me of her, by the way."

"What do you mean?"

"Well, you are a beautiful woman, very fit, intelligent, and are family oriented. I have also begun to see your wit at work." "Thank you for the compliments, Maria. Coming from a person whose attributes even exceed those you described is pretty special. By the way, I have found talking with Father Tony to be extremely comforting, and I guess I just wondered how we would have gotten along before he entered the ministry."

7

Just before noon on the day before he was to leave for Curacao, Father Tony was visited in his role as chaplain by Andy Miller.

"Listen, Father, my mother and I have decided to keep our information within the family. We are trying to help my brother ourselves."

"And what about the information you have divulged in confession, can I reveal it to others?"

"No, Father. I hope you understand."

"No, Andy, I don't. You have put me in a very uncomfortable position. You realize that your brother may be responsible for the murder of the woman I was going to marry. Doesn't that matter to you? Don't you want to do what is right? I know that you and your mom must be guilt-ridden because of the knowledge you have."

"Sorry, Father. We want you to adhere to your vow."

The fact that the gun used to murder Angela, albeit accidentally, was no longer an issue that Father Tony could discuss. He had learned that fact during one of Andy Miller's visits to confession. The erudition relative to the father of Alex and Andy Miller's weapon, inclusive of the gun permit and Mrs. Miller's suspicion of her elder son taking it, were off the table. As a civilian not educated in police and legal matter issues, this was devastating to Tony.

Without tying in the gun, I may as well give up on my pursuit for the truth, he thought to himself. *I have no way of bringing up the weapon that may have been used without violating the Seal of Confession.*

8

The Curacao Marriott Beach Resort and Emerald Casino had been described in brochures as "embodying the island's perfect mix of Caribbean and Old Amsterdam charm." Nestled on the beautiful Piscadera Bay, the wedding destination offered expansive ocean views, world-class dining and casino, and the excitement of a scuba diving night right off shore.

The first Curacao evening saw the bride- and groom-to-be spending time with Teresa's sister and brother-in-law and Paul's two best friends and their wives.

"Let Mom hang out with people her own age," bellowed Maria. "It's good for her. She really hasn't done that very often since Dad died."

"You are probably right, sis. That's two good thoughts you have had so far this year, not bad."

Johnny Sullivan was hysterical, the laughter not appreciated at all by his wife.

"Keep laughing, Johnny, and see if you . . ."

Maria paused before completing the sexual reference remark.

"It's OK, Maria, c'mon, sis, what were you going to say? Pretend I am not a priest for the moment."

"I was going to tell him that he would be giving his right hand a lot of exercise tonight."

Donna Banks and her cousin found humor in Maria's pronouncement. Donna gleefully added a response to her stepsister-to-be.

"You are really funny, Maria, and I love the way you two get along together. I see a mutual respect that I believe is very important in a relationship."

Father Tony interjected, smirking, "Wait until you get to know them a little better, Donna. You don't think a Yankees,

Giants, and Ranger fan is always congenial with a Mets, Jets, and Islander fan, do you?"

Christine, Donna's cousin, offered her thoughts on what she deemed to be a fun-filled wedding weekend. "You guys are a riot to hang out with." Just then, Father Carlos joined the group. "Am I too old to be with you folks?"

"Of course not, Father Carlos, please join us," said Maria.

Father Tony was pleased that his friend and confidant joined the gathering. Soon his admonition for Father Carlos to tell a joke was met with some concern.

"Maybe a little later, after a glass of cognac. Would anyone care to join me at the beach bar?"

Maria, Johnny, Donna, Christine, and Father Tony all took the Catholic priest, now a month shy of his fifty-second birthday, up on his invitation.

An hour later, it was Father Carlos who offered the group a chance to share a joke from his extensive repertoire.

"Now remember everyone, this will be the extent of my attempt to emulate Jay Leno. Please excuse me from what you are about to hear. I have a dispensation from my Bishop to tell one such joke a year without repercussion."

Father Tony had heard many of the humorous yarns of the elder priest but never one that required a so-called special exemption. He questioned whether the second glass of cognac had inhibited his ability to remain erudite.

"Are you OK, Father Carlos?"

The priest's positive acknowledgement was accepted with concern by Father Tony.

"I think you have had enough to drink, though. I've never seen you have more than one."

Father Carlos agreed and began his comedic yarn.

"Two golfers, one Irish and one Italian, find an empty bottle while looking for the wayward golf ball hit by the latter. Although it was the Italian who had rubbed the glass container that summoned the appearance of a genie, the magnanimous apparition offers each golfer one wish. Sean requests that when he urinates, the resultant liquid be a fine Irish whiskey, while Enzo, in similar fashion, requests that red wine be the result of his expulsion. That evening, Sean summons his lovely wife and tells her to bring two glasses. He fills each from his manhood and takes a sip from his glass and, smiling, advises his wife to do the same. They enjoy the Irish whiskey and then make love. The next two evenings, the actions are repeated. Four days later, Sean meets his Italian friend at their favorite tavern for happy hour and explains how he and his wife have enjoyed a glass of whiskey and then were intimate on each of the prior three evenings. Enzo is amazed since he also had requested his wife to bring two glasses the first night, and after the initial test, each enjoyed their vino and then made love. On the second night, the couple repeated their exploits.

"'What about last night?' asked, Sean "'Well, I told Rosa to only bring one glass this time.'

"'Why?'

"'I told her she could drink straight from the bottle!'"

There was amazement in the eyes of all five listeners, the sexual reference of the punch line never anticipated. A brief moment of silence was followed by raucous laughter.

Father Tony abruptly announced, "I think I will walk back to the room with Father Carlos. The cognac has him in a twilight zone state. He has spoken his final words for the evening."

As the priests departed for their room, a duo arrived and observed the pleasantry of the evening.

"Jeremy, you made it."

Donna Banks welcomed her brother, Jeremy Bathgate, and his girlfriend, Emily.

Jeremy questioned Father Tony, "Where are you going, I just get here and you are leaving?"

"Hi, Jeremy, it's good to see you." Then acknowledging his girlfriend, "It's nice to meet you, Emily. Say hello to Father Carlos. I am taking him back to our room. I'll be back in fifteen minutes."

"I hope so," uttered the newest female member of the group. "Jeremy has told me a lot about you. I would welcome the opportunity to speak to you personally."

"Certainly, Emily."

Donna Banks looked askance toward her brother's cute and petite girlfriend.

Father Tony's return was brief. He sensed a little tension between Emily and Donna, the latter upset that her time with the priest was compromised by the company of her brother's wedding escort. He felt it best to politely indicate that the on- site gambling casino required his presence.

"Excuse me, everyone, but the blackjack tables await my visitation. I will see you all in the morning. God bless."

9

The exchanging of vows between Teresa Calabrese and Paul Bathgate was staged where the palm trees and rolling surf provided a tranquil and breathtaking commencement of their new life together.

Father Carlos welcomed the throng of some fifty family and friends. The priest was commissioned as the initial representative for the ceremony since Father Tony had the responsibility of accompanying his mother to the altar prior to joining Father Carlos to perform the wedding service.

Maria Calabrese Sullivan, adorned in a turquoise gown, preceded the walk of her mother and brother down the white- sand-laden aisle, while Jeremy Bathgate stood with his father as the designated best man.

Before Tammy Sullivan walked gracefully to the makeshift pulpit for her reading from Corinthians, Father Tony whispered to his mother, "Mom, you look beautiful."

The popular wedding verse from chapter 13 was uttered with the eloquence of an experienced speaker. Johnny Sullivan had tears in his eyes as he listened to his daughter.

> If I speak in human and angelic tongues,
> but do not have love, I am a resounding gong
> or a clashing cymbal.
> And if I have the gift of prophecy and
> comprehend all mysteries and all knowledge;
> if I have all faith so as to move mountains but
> do not have love, I am nothing.
> If I give away everything I own, and if I hand
> my body over so that I may boast but do not
> have love, I gain nothing.
> Love is patient, love is kind. It is not jealous,
> is not pompous and it is not inflated.

It is not rude, it does not seek its own interests, it is not quick-tempered, it does not brood over injury,

It does not rejoice over wrongdoing but rejoices with the truth

Love bears all things, believes all things, hopes all things, endures all things

Faith, hope and love remain. But the greatest of these, is love.

Teresa Calabrese and Paul Bathgate had written their own wedding vows. Neither was privy to what the other had scripted.

A traditional approach was taken by Teresa as she expressed her love and devotion for Paul.

The sixty-six-year-old widower surprised the wedding congregation with his sincere adaption from a popular Paul Simon song.

"Dearest Teresa, from now until the day I leave this earth, I will always be your bridge over troubled water."

When you're weary, feeling small.
When tears are in your eyes, I will dry them all:
I'm on your side. When times get rough
And friends just can't be found,
Like a bridge over troubled water
I will lay me down.
When you're down and out,
When you're on the street,
When evening falls so hard
I will comfort you.
I'll take your part.
When darkness comes
And pain is all around,
Like a bridge over troubled water
I will lay me down.

Taking a line from the Simon and Garfunkel 1970 Grammy Award Song of the Year, what "just can't be found" was a dry eye. Father Tony and his sister, Maria, were sure of one thing: their mother was in good hands.

At the completion of the impeccably arranged wedding ceremony, the congratulations for Mr. and Mrs. Paul Bathgate were a sincere tribute to two widowed grandparents. The throng then found their way to the comfortable outside Marriott hotel surroundings for the cocktail reception. The wedding planner had meticulously included all the recommendations made by Maria and Donna, and the addition of the melodic- singing guitar player, offering soft rock hits of the seventies and eighties, was enthusiastically received.

The wedding toast of the best man, Jeremy, was humorous but a true reflection of respect for his dad. It was also a clear indication of their fully mended relationship. Donna was relieved that her brother made no mention of the family estrangement resulting from his sexual orientation. She kissed and hugged her brother on the completion of his discourse.

"My mother is my hero. She is the glue of the Calabrese family, a person who always finds the best in people and a woman who embodies the 'It is better to give than receive' philosophy. I am so happy that she has met a gentleman like Paul. He is truly the second coming for Mom. I never ever thought I would be saying this to someone other than my father, but I am truly proud to call him Dad."

The concluding remarks of Maria Calabrese Sullivan were met with a thunderous applause. The bride and groom tearfully embraced her. Johnny Sullivan, Tammy, and Tommy soon joined the married couple to heap love on their wife/ mother. Father Anthony Calabrese waited and then went over to his sister.

"Please allow me to take back the remark I made at your tenth birthday party when I called you a chubby, pimple-faced spoiled brat."

"I don't remember that!"

"I said it under my breath."

"Really?"

"Nah, I just made it up. I figured if I didn't tell you that just now, I would be crying like a little kid whose baseball just fell into the storm sewer for the next fifteen minutes. That was just beautiful, sis, you're the greatest."

If a David Letterman–like "ten best" of the event were voted on, the resulting list would have been as follows:

10. Father Carlos's attempting to place his hands out of harms' way while slow dancing with Donna's cousin, Christine.

9. The cutting of the cannoli cake affording Teresa with an opportunity to playfully get Paul with a smear in his face.

8. Jeremy Bathgate announcing his engagement to Emily.

    This caught Donna off guard, but with prompting from Father Tony, she endeavored to be enthusiastic.

7. Paul surprising everyone by having the waiter/ waitresses bring out ten bottles of Dom Pérignon for the champagne toast.

6. A mini dance contest pitting Tammy Sullivan and Scott Banks against Tommy Sullivan and Becky Banks that was interrupted when Father Tony and Donna pushed both young couples aside and lit up the dance floor to that "Old Time Rock and Roll."

5. Maria Sullivan, Donna Banks, and her cousin Christine imitating the Supremes in a fun-filled rendition of "Stop! in the Name of Love."

4. Father Tony and Johnny, as promised, performing their Blues Brothers dance to the thunderous

applause of all. Many Marriott guests who had no connection with the wedding viewed the Jake and Elwood rendition with delight.

3. Paul and his daughter, Donna, dancing to the Beatles' "In My Life."

    Though I know I'll never lose affection
    For people and things that went before
    I know I'll often stop and think about them
    In my life, I Iove you more
    In my life—I love you more.

2. Teresa Calabrese Bathgate and Father Tony as they held each as one, dancing to the Ben E. King classic "Stand by Me."

    When the light has come
    And the land is dark
    And the moon is the only light we'll see
    No, I won't be afraid
    Oh, I won't be afraid
    Just as long as you stand, stand by me.

1. The bride and groom fooling everyone by commencing their first dance together with some raucous strutting to the Bill Haley classic "Rock around the Clock" before transitioning to Frankie Valle's "Can't Take My Eyes Off You."

    Pardon the way that I stare, there's nothing else to compare
    The thought of you leaves me weak, there are no words left to speak
    But if you feel like I feel, oh, then let me know it's real
    You're just too good to be true, can't take my eyes off of you.

10

The late Saturday afternoon Bathgate-Calabrese wedding Mass on the beach had fulfilled the Sunday obligation of the attending Catholics. This was fortunate as the consumption of liquid spirits by the majority of the guests resulted in their inability to fully function on Sunday morning.

Father Anthony Calabrese was in his element at the wedding. His ability to party was not diminished by his years in the priesthood. He could dance, he could drink, and he loved being with family and friends. The release from thinking about adherence to his vows was as welcome as the recollection of the many dominant pitching performances he relished in his years in high school and college.

Listening to the deafening snoring of Father Carlos was humorous to him at first. Then the persistence of the strident sounds prevented him from sleeping. He decided to dress and take a walk on the beach as the hotel room digital timepiece adjacent to his bed read 6:53 a.m.

His bare feet altered a path along the parting of the shoreline waves and the pristine beach sand. He recalled similar walks at both Rockaway Beach in Queens and his excursions to Jones Beach on Long Island. His thoughts then focused on a vision of Angela Santino and how she adorned a bathing suit in similar fashion to a Sports Illustrated model. The recollection caused tears to appear; the soft Caribbean breezes quelled the flow from his eyes, and a passerby might ascertain the moisture to merely be mist from the ocean. Tony looked skyward as other contemplations invaded his thinking. He knew he would be without a roommate that evening and that the temptation of Donna Banks may surface. He wondered about Alex Miller. Had he killed Angela? If he found that to be a fact, would he divulge such information in violation of his vows?

Father Tony arrived back at his room at 8:20 a.m. Father Carlos had just begun to stir.

"Rise and shine, Father Carlos, time to get dressed and have some breakfast."

"Fifteen more minutes, Father Tony. Then I will shower, get dressed, and pack. I am looking forward to having a large glass of orange juice and tea. My breakfast cuisine will include bacon, eggs, hash browns, and whole wheat toast."

"OK, but I am going over now. I need my morning caffeine hit. I'll see you there. Remember, your flight is at noon, and you will need to be there at least an hour before, so don't dawdle." Father Tony had another reason for his abrupt departure.

Coffee was just a cover for his promise to Donna to meet at eight thirty. He hoped that her cousin, Christine, would be as tardy as Father Carlos.

The priest added a pair of sandals to his shorts and Yankees T-shirt wardrobe. The outside breakfast area of the Marriott was replete with round tables, most typically adorned with an umbrella and four wicker chairs.

He situated himself facing the area where guests would enter and beckoned a waitress with a polite smile and wave of his hand.

"Good morning. How are you today?"

"Good morning, sir, my name is Angela, what can I get for you?" Father Tony observed a lovely young girl, whom he guessed was in her late teens. Fortunately, her name did not elicit thoughts of his former slain fiancée. The waitress had no resemblance to the girl he referred to as Hoops; her hair was reddish blond, and she was about six inches shorter. "I would love a cup of coffee, Angela. Thank you."

Before the waitress departed, he noticed Donna walking toward his table.

"Hold on, Angela, can you see what the lady would like?"

"Just coffee for now, please." "Yes, miss."

Donna took a seat across from Tony. The gleam from her radiant white teeth was conspicuous as she spoke. "Well, if it isn't Jake Blues, or maybe I should call you John Travolta."

Father Tony was not the type to be embarrassed, but in this case, a slight redness to his cheeks became apparent.

"I wish I had a rebuttal and could indicate a woman entertainer who was your equal on the dance floor, but I don't think there is one. You move like a gazelle, and having fun doing it is just so evident. I loved dancing with you."

"Well, thank you, John."

"Enough of the John Travolta analogy, Ms. Banks," said a grinning priest."

"It's ironic, John Travolta played Tony Manero in *Saturday Night Fever*, so I guess I can just call you Tony. Oh, sorry, Father, I meant to say Father Tony."

The deliberation of the cleric was one that would jeopardize his true feelings about Donna, perhaps even threatening his vow of celibacy. He welcomed the distraction of Angela, the waitress, that is, returning with a pot of coffee. He poured a cup for Donna and one for himself.

"How do you take it, Donna?" "The coffee?"

"You are in a mischievous mood I see, yes, stepsister, the coffee."

"My God, I think I am the only girl alive to have a bisexual brother and a stepbrother who is a priest."

"Why did you bring that up about Jeremy? He just got engaged last night. Aren't you happy for him?"

"I am sorry, Father. That was wrong. I love Jeremy, but I have doubts about whether Emily is the right girl for him."

"I spoke with him last night. He loves her, Donna. Be there for him, he needs your support."

"Yes, Father Tony, you're right. I will be there for Jeremy. I just have other things on my mind."

The magnetism between the two was reminiscent of the last evening on the cruise. It far surpassed a platonic relationship of stepsister and stepbrother. Yet Father Tony remained composed until Donna could not withhold her innermost thoughts.

"I think that I am falling in love with you, Father."

The priest had a reprieve as Christine and Father Carlos arrived simultaneously. The conversation was now among four adults, two of which had a mutual attraction that had grown beyond the resolve of either to control.

11

Father Tony joined his mother, stepfather, sister, brother-in-law, and stepsister in thanking Father Carlos for his administering to the wedding Mass. Mrs. Teresa Bathgate hugged the priest and was teary eyed as she also thanked him for years of "being there" for her family. Maria Sullivan added a funny quip about the priest's difficulty in his slow dance technique the previous evening.

"One hand in front and the second gently on the hip, Father, and you'll never get in trouble."

The Marriott van departed for the airport at 10:25 a.m.

"It was so wonderful to have Father Carlos there yesterday, and then to be so fortunate to have a second priest, my son, no less, was more than any woman could ask for in a wedding ceremony."

"We are blessed, Teresa," added Paul. "We are most definitely blessed."

Father Tony was now a single man, that is, relative to having a hotel room companion. The realization that his solitary confinement may be threatened by a sultry figure that evening loomed.

Paul Bathgate walked back to the hotel lobby with Father Tony. Both sought a newspaper to get caught up with events from the States.

"You are quite a dancer, Father. I've never seen anyone who could keep up with Donna before."

"I can see why, Paul. She is fantastic. You don't mind if I call you Paul, do you?"

"Certainly not, Father Tony, that's fine with me."

"Listen, Paul, my mother adores you, and I know you will always be there for her. I am happy to be your stepson. I also want to congratulate you on Jeremy's engagement."

"I hope that works out for him."

"It will, Paul, trust me on this, it will."

A copy of the early edition of the *New York Times* and *New York Daily News* were purchased, the former the choice of Paul Bathgate.

"I've got it, Father," handing the gift store worker a ten-dollar bill and collecting his change. "Father Tony, this is difficult for me to say but . . ."

Paul Bathgate paused and placed his right hand on the shoulder of the priest.

"I think my daughter is in love with you."

12

At the poolside bar early that afternoon, Father Anthony Calabrese was deluged with feelings that far surpassed his ability to cope with. The Seal of Confession regarding Angela's murder and his posture with regard to Donna Banks, particularly in light of her and her father's identifications that morning, had him in a quandary.

"Barry, let me have an extra dry Grey Goose martini on the rocks with olives."

"Just wave the cork, Father?

"You got that right."

"I have the olives filled with blue cheese if you'd like."
"Great, Barry, put five of them in there."

As he was about to order his second drink, Father Tony was joined by Jeremy Bathgate and Johnny Sullivan. The two had made a strong connection at the wedding reception, sharing procedures of the San Francisco and New York Police Departments.

"What are you guys having? You need to catch up with me, and a toast to Jeremy is in order."

Jeremy was not bashful. "Let me have a Jack Daniel's on the rocks."

"Make mine a Heineken with a shot of Jamison's. That will give me the resolve not to tell your sister off for making fun of my endeavor for fifteen minutes of fame when she prevented me from singing 'Danny Boy' last night."

Father Tony and Jeremy laughed at the Detective's pronouncement, with Jeremy adding that Johnny's demonstration of his Elwood Blues dance floor moves should have qualified him for the Hollywood Walk of Fame and that there was no reason for further adulation.

"What about your favorite priest, Jeremy? Didn't you like my John Belushi rendition?"

"Of course, Father Tony, you can be next to Johnny along the Hollywood Walk."

Soon the priest was discussing events, already known to his brother-n-law, with Jeremy. He concluded that a second opinion regarding Angela's murder couldn't hurt. Then he offered a new angle to Johnny for consideration.

"Listen, Sully, I have information on a weapon that I believe was used to kill Angela. I will be violating my vow as a priest if I tell you, though."

Johnny Sullivan sought to protect his brother-in-law if he possibly could. "Can't you give me a clue without violating the vow?"

"No."

13

After dinner that evening, Father Tony and Donna walked together, following Maria and Johnny along the beach. The married couple held hands as the trailing duo strolled and conversed.

"Father Tony, what's on your mind? You can share anything with me."

"What's on my mind? Now that would take some time to get through, Donna. Where would you like me to start?"

He decided to discuss the events of some fourteen years prior, the initial life-altering occurrence that eventually led him to the priesthood. By the time he revealed that he had recently learned that Angela had been shot in the heart and that he might know who had killed her, he sobbed.

Donna consoled him and was soon joined by Maria and Johnny, who recognized that he was in distress.

"Maria, I'll head back with your brother. Why don't you and Johnny just continue your walk and relax."

As the two made their way back to the Marriott, room 107, the quarters of the priest, Father Tony gently placed his right hand behind the neck of his escort.

"Listen, Donna, if I invite you in, we both know what will happen. I think that it would be for the best if you leave."

Chapter X

Embryonic Development

1

The early foray into the 2001 season for the St. John the Baptist Vikings was a success. The team record was unblemished, following a weekday evening victory.

The travel baseball team games provided the conflicted cleric with an outlet to avoid thinking about his quest for the truth regarding the events on St. Patrick's Day eve in 1987.

The team record stood at 5–0 prior to the commencement of the scheduled late Saturday morning encounter. His nephew, stepsister's son, his assistant coach brother-in-law, and his scorekeeper/administrative assistant, the woman who occupied a preponderance of his thoughts as he lay in bed at night, were all ecstatic at the team's previous results.

During batting practice, Father Tony had a lengthy conversation with Beverly Thomas, whose son remained as a key ballplayer on the team.

"Hi, Father, I like being undefeated. My husband, Jerry, said to say hello."

"How is he, Beverly?"

"Great, Father, just great, and our whole family can't thank you enough."

"Happy to hear that, Beverly, give him my regards." "By the way, Father, your scorekeeper is very nice."

The catholic priest was not sure of Beverly's thought process relative to the comment about the woman he was so attracted to. His response diverted the need for further discussion.

"You know that my mom just married her dad, right? She is now my stepsister."

Father Tony noticed that Johnny was not his jovial self after the game, a 9–2 victory, and sought to spur his spirits.

"C'mon, Johnny, where's the team spirit? It's time for celebration. Let's take the boys for pizza and sodas, what do you say?"

The comments had little impact on the police detective.

"I was able to get a copy of the medical examiner report for Angela from the night of her shooting. Remember, you asked me to try to get my hands on it. I pulled some strings, and I have it in my glove compartment. I wanted to wait until after the game to give it to you."

"Thanks, Sully, I am glad you were able to get it without me having to involve Angela's parents. Is there a problem?"

"Just take a look at it when you get back to the rectory, not before."

Father Tony was puzzled but had promised the boys pizza if they won. He lost a little of his enthusiasm but remained upbeat as he made the pizza parlor toast.

"That's six in a row, guys. Great job everyone. V-I-K-I-N-G-S, Vikings, Vikings, Vikings!"

2

Father Tony arrived back at the rectory at 2:35 p.m. He was scheduled to hear confessions at four o'clock. A shower and the reading of the medical examiner report were on his agenda before listening to the sins of his congregation.

Tony dried off and put on a robe and slippers. He checked his watch, 2:50 p.m. He meandered to his desk and picked up the manila envelope he received from his brother-in-law. It was carefully sealed, and he sought the letter opener for assistance. Tony perused the document. What was so disturbing to Johnny that caused him to be so somber?

The identification that the bullet had entered Angela through the heart and that her death came within thirty seconds brought tears to Tony's eyes. The report was thrown on the desk. The phrase "It should have been me" was repeated several times. A few minutes of sobbing preceded the continued examination of the document.

Tony took a yellow magic marker and scrolled over the information regarding the bullet description. Could it have come from the gun owned by the father of Andy and Alex Miller? How could he discuss that with Johnny without violating his vow? Could Jeremy Bathgate assist him with his forensic background, and could he make the request without disclosure of his actual intent?

He decided to put the report down and leave for the confessional.

3

Although Father Tony had not regained his composure, the fulfillment of his duties as a Catholic priest remained important to him. He sat in the confessional at 4:00 p.m., awaiting the initial penitent.

He questioned whether the hatred that filled his thought process made him worthy to accept the words "Bless me, Father." *How can I be a blessing others? I am the one who needs the blessing.*

Then, the voice of a young girl, not more than ten years old, he guessed, captured his attention. After her "Bless me, Father" introduction, which included that it had been a mere two weeks since her last confession, the juvenile rattled off several sins, venial in nature, and then asked for what she deemed to be a "special" blessing.

"It's me, Father Tony, Cecilia. My brother, Timothy, plays on your travel team. You played catch with me a few times, remember?"

"Yes, Cecilia, I do. How can I help you?"

"I have been diagnosed with leukemia, Father, and I cursed Jesus for letting me get it. I am so sorry. I know that there are many other kids with diseases worse than mine and that I should be asking Jesus to help make me better rather than feeling sorry for myself."

The earnest remark was the tonic Tony needed to assuage his own feelings of hatred. The priest spent the next five minutes comforting the young girl. He had tears in his eyes as he concluded his remarks.

"Thank you for sharing your feelings with me, Cecilia. God bless you. I will be praying for you. Remember that Jesus will always be with you."

Upon completion of his priestly duties in the confessional, Father Tony returned to his room at the rectory. He changed into a more casual wardrobe before grabbing a pad and pen.

His mission was to be erudite with regard to a future course of action. Tony labeled the top of the page Facts Learned and underlined the words. Then the mentally embattled parish priest drew a line down the middle of the page, such that he would be able to develop two distinct columns below his selected heading. The left side would include facts learned in the confessional, which would therefore bind him to his vow of nondisclosure, i.e., the Seal of Confession. To the right of the line, he would list findings from his discussions and observations made outside of the boundaries of the Seal.

Soon both columns were filled with critical facts, and he studied them for a few minutes. His compulsion was then to re-review the medical examiner's report. He was curious as to why Johnny was reluctant to discuss the information it included. *There is nothing in here that I didn't already know, except that Angela had expired within thirty seconds of being shot,* he thought to himself.

There were a few handwritten notations toward the bottom of the page that he had previously merely scanned. On closer inspection, he found one such comment confusing. It was a medical description with an * adjacent to it.

The scripted phrase of the medical examiner concluded with words he read several times.

"Embryonic development estimated at three weeks."

Anthony Calabrese read it one more time. "Embryonic development?"

"Oh Lord Jesus, no. Please, Lord, please tell me no. Angela was pregnant?"

The realization that the St. Patrick's Day shooting not only caused the loss of the woman he cherished but also prevented Angela and him from being parents was much more than Father Anthony Calabrese could bear. He cried out loudly several times as he wept.

"*No*, Please, Lord, *no!*"

Several hours in the chapel praying did little to dispel Tony's anguish. He recalled discussions of parenthood with Angela.

"Listen, Tony, if you do ever come across with that ring and we get married, I'll pick our first child's name if we have a boy.

You can have the honor for a baby girl. I am leaning to Marc Joseph or Scott Vincent."

The pleasant memory was ephemeral. Hatred and retribution soon pervaded his thoughts. Clemency was seemingly off the table as he wept.

"If I prove Alex Miller killed Angela and my child, maybe I should kill him. An eye for an eye."

4

"Sully, its Father Tony. Now I know why you were reluctant to give me the medical examiner report. Last night was very tough for me. Listen, I'll be coming over early tomorrow for dinner. Do you think we could meet at twelve thirty? I have several questions I would like to bounce off you."

"Father Tony, just so you know, I cried myself when I learned Angela was pregnant when she was killed. I'll see you at twelve thirty."

The answers to his questions would clarify how the tormented minister of faith would proceed in his mission to come to grips with the murder of Angela Santino, the woman he expected to spend the remainder of his life with. The medical examiner report revelation that Angela was shot in the heart and, of ultimate significance, that she was three weeks with child were near impossible for him to cope with.

Could Detective Johnny Sullivan

- meet with the parents of the two boys shot by Alex Miller during the Sheepshead Bay robbery and inquire as to any recollection they had of the older person who was often seen with the high school students?
- talk with Andy Miller to discuss what he might know about his brother?
- review the personnel file of Alex Miller for other incidents involving his response to liquor store robberies?

The priest reasoned that these inquiries could be made without violation to his Seal of Confession vow. He debated whether he should confirm his conclusions with Father Carlos but decided not to.

By the time Tony reached the house the following afternoon, he had a change of plan.

"Listen, Sully. Let's not talk today. I don't want to spoil dinner for everyone. I know my mother wants to show us the pictures from her honeymoon week on Curacao. Can you meet later this week?"

"No problem, Father Tony."

5

"Hi, Father Tony, it's Donna. I just wanted to call to see how you were. I noticed that you weren't yourself yesterday. I hope you know that I am here for you."

"Thank you, Donna, I do have a lot on my mind."

"Well, I can't cook anywhere near as well as your mother or Maria, but I make a mean tuna salad. Would you like to come over for lunch?"

"I have to visit an elderly couple who recently lost their daughter to cancer and asked to speak with me. I can probably make it to your house by one."

Donna had tuna on rye sandwiches, pickles, and potato chips ready on the priest's arrival. What she didn't have ready was a way to console Father Tony after he revealed what he had learned from the medical examiner report. That is, with words. She hugged Tony and pressed her body against his, and the man of the cloth initially refrained from a sexual response.

Donna took a step backward.

"I love you, Father Tony. Let me be there for you."

Father Anthony Calabrese responded. Words that Donna had hoped to hear for months were uttered.

"I love you too, Donna."

A stepsister has probably never run into the arms of a stepbrother, particularly an ordained catholic priest, any faster. They embraced, and Tony took Donna by the hand.

"Where is your bedroom, Donna? I want to be with you."

Tony was soon displaying his prowess in love making; fourteen years of abstinence did not prevent the return of the Italian Stallion.

The movements were without haste, gradually ramping as he rounded the bases. Perhaps he was following the Meat Loaf refrain in their hit "Paradise by the Dashboard Light."

We're gonna go all the way tonight
We're gonna go all the way
And tonight's the night.

Actually, the priest had his own script, a scenario that he had often repeated with Angela Santino.

The French had nothing on Tony regarding the use of the muscular organ in his mouth, and the fondling and then sucking on her firm and ample breasts ensued. Donna was moaning with desire even before Tony's finger entered her vagina. His insertion was with knowledge of location, and soon the words "Oh my God, Father Tony" were proclaimed. The placement of the cleric's tongue on her clitoris and unshaved pussy elicited an orgasmic reaction. Donna then moved to a dominant position, and Tony entered her from below. The thrusts were powerful and yet passionate.

Donna rested her head on Father Tony's chest at the conclusion of the episode. He was comforted and at peace. This was not a sexual encounter for either partner but rather an expression of their mutual love.

6

How sacred is the vow of a priest to withhold disclosure of facts deemed to be instrumental in solving a crime? What about the involvement of a murder? What about the murder of a woman whom you expected to be with forever? How do you remain silent when the murder took two lives, the second your unborn child?

Father Anthony Calabrese struggled with this dilemma, often wondering if his Seal of Confession commitment was fair and usually concluding that it was not. It was obvious to him that without permission to reveal his cognizance about the weapon owned by the father of Andy and Alex Miller, a gun he believed to be the instrument of Angela's death, his ability to uncover the truth was thwarted.

Father Tony had a thought on how to move forward. He would reach out to the mother of the Miller brothers, a woman whom he had provided comfort to during his bereavement group sessions.

The meetings at St. John the Baptist parish required each participant to leave a phone number. The 718 area code was the same as the church landline number, so the dialing of 759- 3457 sufficed.

"Hello, Mrs. Miller, this is Father Tony from St. John the Baptist, how are you?"

"How wonderful to hear from you, Father. I hope you are well. I will always be grateful for your compassion during my attendance of your meetings. What can I do for you?"

"I was hoping to have you speak with Andy about identifications he has made to me in the confessional. Issues he has discussed with you. Would you do that for me?"

There was a pause and what sounded to Father Tony like a deep breath.

"My son Andy and I have decided not to speak further about anything involving Alex. I am sorry, Father, but that is our decision. God bless you, Father Tony, but that is our final answer on the subject."

The police file reviewed by Johnny Sullivan had revealed that the bullets retrieved from the bodies of Angela Santino and the son of the Bay Ridge liquor store owner matched those of ejection from a .38 revolver. This fact meant nothing on its own merit. The question of whether the gun owned by the Miller family was equivalent remained unanswered. The gun permit held by Alex Miller would solve that dilemma, but how would its retrieval be possible for the priest?

"Please, Lord, show me the way."

Chapter XI

No, Just Tony

1

Patrolman Alex Miller was brought into custody on Monday, June 25, 2001. The arrest by Detective Johnny Sullivan was, according to the district attorney's office, based on sound evidence, with charges filed for grand theft and murder in the first degree.

The extensive investigation of Alex Miller was prompted by insider information that Sullivan received from an unnamed source. The murders of two teenagers during a Sheepshead Bay liquor store robbery in late 2000 was linked to over a dozen unsolved liquor store thefts in the five boroughs of New York City dating back to 1998.

Miller was identified as the mastermind behind the robberies, accused of soliciting reputable and intelligent high school students to perform the burglaries. The police officer was deemed to have provided his young cohorts with the details on key shipments of expensive liquors, the date and time to perform the break-in under the least possible resistance, and armed the teenagers with weapons. It was determined that Miller shot the teens because of the botched robbery attempt for fear that the two would implicate him after being caught.

Patrolman Andrew Miller, younger brother of the indicted officer of eight years, had reluctantly turned over a copy of a gun permit under the threat of obstruction of justice. The revelation of the .38 caliber revolver, once owned by their father, proved to be the key to the arrest of his brother and was the missing link in the resolution of the Cold Case of a 1987 liquor store robbery and murder in Bay Ridge, Brooklyn, for which Detective Sullivan earned a special commendation from the NYPD Police Commissioner.

2

"Bless me, Father, for I have sinned." Father Carlos listened intently. His protégé, so to speak, Father Anthony Calabrese, was confessing to transgressions related to his violation of the Seal of Confession. The weekday confession was a special request by Father Tony, the day following the arrest of the murderer of Angela Santino.

The priest, ordained in 1993, provided his mentor with a surprise.

"I am no longer a believer in the mandates of the Church relative to the Seal of Confession. I did not feel that I should be prevented from disclosing facts that would convict a murderer. I revealed everything I knew to my brother-in-law, Father Carlos, and I have no regrets."

Father Anthony Calabrese continued his transparent confession.

"I do not believe that I can in good faith continue to serve the church, Father Carlos. I have decided to leave the priesthood." "No, Anthony, I advise you to give this some time. Please spend the evening in prayer. Then, we can meet for lunch tomorrow to discuss it further."

That evening, sadness pervaded Tony's thoughts. He realized that the joy and sense of fulfillment received from his priestly ministry might end. He prayed for several hours.

3

The lunch meeting was helpful to Father Tony. Father Carlos encouraged him to continue praying and offered the reasons why the priesthood would provide him a life of fulfillment.

"You have assisted countless parishioners at St. John the Baptist. I strongly encourage you to ask the Lord for guidance and be patient. This decision should not be made in haste."

"Father Carlos, I should have confessed this to you yesterday. Please accept this disclosure now. I succumbed to temptation and violated my vow of chastity."

"Was this transgression with your stepsister?"

"Yes, Father. I am in love with her and feel that I can no longer suppress my desire to be with her."

4

Teresa Calabrese Bathgate temporarily remained at her home in the borough of Queens, New York City. An upscale senior living condominium complex in Nassau County would soon become the residence of Mr. and Mrs. Paul Bathgate.

Father Tony was uneasy as he arrived. He was unsure of how the disclosure of the potential for him to return to the life of a lay person would be received by his mother and sister.

The two women, with whom Anthony Calabrese could always converse with since childhood, cried uncontrollably upon his disclosure that Angela Santino was with child on the evening of her murder.

"Listen, Ma, after I learned that Angela was pregnant with our child, everything changed for me. I felt I was restricted by a vow that made no sense. I wound up telling Johnny everything I knew about facts I learned in the confessional. I violated the Seal of Confession. That's how he was able to charge Alex Miller."

Tony then explained that he was also unfaithful to his vow of chastity and that he was in love with Donna Banks.

"We've had a special connection ever since the cruise. I tried to curtail my feelings, but in Curacao, the mutual attraction became increasingly difficult to resist. I was able to avoid succumbing to temptation, but, Ma, my feelings far surpassed sexual desires. I knew that I was truly in love with her."

Then switching his attention directly toward Maria, "Leaving the priesthood may be something I need to do, sis. I just don't believe I can fulfill my vows any longer."

"Does Father Carlos know about this, Anthony?" inquired his mother.

"Yes, Ma."

"What about Donna, does she know you are leaving the priesthood?" added Maria.

"Not yet."

5

After the full disclosure to his mother and sister, Father Tony called Donna and indicated he would be at her house at noon the following day.

"I have something I need to talk to you about."

The alluring lass also had no inkling as to what she was about to hear that afternoon. After sharing the large Italian hero and one-half-pound of potato salad that he had brought, supplemented by two sixteen-ounce Diet Cokes from Donna's refrigerator, the priest diverted from their conversation about the New York Yankees.

"I can't do this anymore, Donna."

"What? Tell me why. I thought you said you loved me."

"No, Donna, that is not it. I want to leave the priesthood. I am living a lie."

"What does that mean for me, Father Tony?"

Five minutes later, the two were passionately making love.

6

Father Tony was assisted by his brother-in-law, niece, and nephew as all his belongings were moved from his room at the rectory to his old bedroom on the first floor of the house where he was born. Soon, he would occupy the first level of the brick-faced structure himself, that is, except that he would share space with a female Lab/Golden Retriever mix, Seven.

The questions of the trio were countless. It seemed as if Johnny, Tammy, and Tommy took turns in their quest for answers, many of which the soon-to-be ex-priest had no appropriate response for. He did his best to make several issues clear. The knowledge of Angela having been killed while carrying his child was an overwhelming burden for him. He felt no qualms about revealing the facts that, as a priest, he had vowed never to divulge. His feelings for Donna Banks were authentic, similar to those dating back to 1987.

After an hour or so, Tony was left alone, and he began to hang several pictures in his room, many of which had been displayed at his rectory abode. He perused the picture that portrayed the image of Thurman Munson on the Yankee Stadium center field screen with his teammate Graig Nettles looking on. It was just a few days after the All-Star catcher had perished in a plane crash. It was a sad time for Tony; Munson was his boyhood favorite. Prior to the death of Angela and his dad, the tragedy affected him more than any other.

He then chuckled at the recollection of having received a framed photo of Don Mattingly being pursued at home plate by Morganna. The buxom Kissing Bandit and Mattingly portrayal was a present from Angela but was never displayed at his church domicile since he felt it was inappropriate. He laughed as he read the card from her that accompanied the picture.

"Maybe she has a bigger chest, but I have a nicer ass."

I'll put the card away and just hang the picture, he thought to himself.

Tony decided in the affirmative with regard to hanging several photos of his dad, several of which included his mom, sister, and himself. He opted to put away his photos of Angela, theorizing that they might be upsetting to Donna.

7

Anthony Calabrese entered Christina's Jewelry store, an establishment where his family had shopped dating back to the late sixties.

The daughter of the woman whose name appeared on the two-foot-by-four-foot sign hanging above the entrance greeted him warmly as he made his way toward the counter.

"Hi, Father Tony, I haven't seen you since before Christmas. Your sister has been in several times. How have you been?"

"Well, Brigid, a lot has happened." "Tell me, Father Tony, I am all ears."

"I am no longer Father Tony, Brigid, just Tony."

An explanation of his transition from priest to layperson was surprising to the woman he had known since both were teenagers.

"Listen, Brigid, I have $7,500 to spend. Show me what you have in diamond engagement rings."

Fini